ACKNOWLEDGEMENTS

I would like to give thanks to:

Jeremy Poynting, for his indefatigable patience and unparalleled editing. I'm grateful.

Jacob Ross, for his commitment to this work and for passing on a true love of words. Passion is everything.

My parents, for the love of a good story, shared.

Family and friends, whose support and unwavering belief in me, helped this book to be.

To the Peepal Tree Family, one love and respect to all.

Dedicated to my mum, who keeps giving me life and to all the lives within.

DESIREE REYNOLDS

SEDUCE

PEEPAL TREE

First published in Great Britain in 2013
Peepal Tree Press Ltd
17 King's Avenue
Leeds LS6 1QS
England

ISBN13: 9781845232177

DI CAST

Time: Some time ago, before yuh barn.
Place: Church Island, a two-bit rock off di mainlan

In order of appearance

Hyacinth Collins: Pastor Collins' mumma, good lady of the church, guardian of everybody's morals, a nosey ole bat.

Alfredo: Town postmaster, a black man, married to dat brown woman, Clementina.

Clementina: Wife to Alfredo, a self-righteous woman, too conscious of she status.

Mikey: Ole Rasta, ole soljah, Seduce lover; him spend time ah foreign.

Glory: Seduce darta, yellow woman who tink she betta dan odda people.

The Lampis: Seduce good fren an sistahs in faith. Women who cook a fish call lampi, which use to get nyam all over di worl but nobody want it now. Many a Lampi had to turn prostitute to live. Dey keep di ole ways alive. Dem outside Seduce house, for Glory don't want dem in dere.

Pastor Collins: Hyacinth Collins' pickney, a minister. Him have him own church dats respectable an too quiet. Him don't believe in di ole ways.

Seduce: Jus dead. Glory mumma, Loo an Son granmumma, a onetime Lampi.

Marshall: Head of police roun dese parts. A brown man, him fight in di firs worl war. He tink him hol' all di power roun ya. Him no know how him feel bout Seduce.

Loo: Seduce grandarta, Glory darta and Son sistah. Her farda name Jono, a sailor from di mainlan. No one know what happen to him. Loo name afta Lucretia, a legend roun yah, from slavery time. Loo always talk seh we an us, for she have more dan one spirit in she body.

Honey Rock: Loo's name fi one ah dem back to Africa man, a smooth-skin, virgin politician, choosing Church fi free. She meet im at di rally outside ah di courthouse.

Son: Seduce granson, Glory son an Loo brodder. Him a teacher pan di mainlan.

People not here any more

Big Pearl Before Swine: Seduce granmumma.
Likkle Pearl Before Swine: Seduce mumma.
Geno: Seduce los' bwoy pickney.

FIRST MOVEMENT

In and around Seduce's House

Beginnings

The day opens her legs to let the night in. It moves from a dark lilac to bottomless purple. You wait for a moment to adjust your eyes and against your skin is a smooth coolness. By the light of the moon, you can make out a large structure that almost blots out the horizon. You can't tell if it's a building or something more natural, a shadow, a greater darkness just recognisable against the blackness. Clinging to the edges you can see movement.

The souls sail around, chit-chatting and remembering nothing. Souls do that. Visiting so many places, so many people that they very soon forget where they have been. They only know where they are going, and when they are there have already started to forget. They wheel overhead and cry loud into the dark, feathers reflecting moonlight, sharp eyes watchful. They bustle and nudge each other, some getting angry about the lack of space. A few circle around, waiting for one to go back. Sometimes they nip and scratch. They know they are only there for a short time, so they want to make the most of it. Some are bigger than others, some are quiet but most are loud and, for those that can hear them, their squawking can be heard for miles. Their long claws grip tightly to the perches and their small eyes look as if they are trying to remember.

A gap on the branch becomes free and several souls race for it. A fight breaks out, as it often does at such times.

They wait. They never know exactly when it's going to happen, that strong tugging that takes them back. Through the light and the dark, the cold and the heat, and finally again the cold. Like mothers, they forget the pain. A small one manages to beat others off the perch. This one has been waiting for the pull back. Wants to go. Looking, waiting, watching. Others are squawking loudly.

She pays them no mind, she has squawks of her own she's not ready to let go of. Sounds and trills. But she is tired and ready to get back.

Hyacinth

"Praise Jesus, our Farder, sweet Lord, in Jesus name, amen! What a sad time it is for all ah we. Here to bury di good sister. Now, we know dat *all* truths will be reveal before him. We are naked in di eyes of di Lord. All secrets will be reveal, amen! Let me hear an amen! When we walk in di light of God, we walk without sin, we walk in His righteousness. We will be flesh of His flesh, blood of Him blood. But if you sin, you will be cast out by di livin God. We not talkin bout di sun, moon an stars, like dem heathens outside. Close you eyes, close dem, feel God move in dis room, feel him, lock out di filth and wantonness outside dis house, amen. The Lord protect him sheep and let di evil doers be dash into di fiery pits of hell... Me an dis woman had our time, oh yes. It's true. Dey may not have been any love lost but we respec each odda, yes dere was respect..."

... Me come fi mek sure di ole bitch dead. Me never like her – dutty, filthy woman. Mek me sick. What all dese women doing here? No decent law-abiding woman should be sullied by attending dis travesty and disgrace. Me? Like me seh, me hear dat she get tek, an me come fi mek sure she gone. What is wrong wid my boy? What to do? Him shoulda refuse to do di ceremony. Him should perform some kinda test. Mek sure di ole whore pass. Me not sure. You hear bout dese people? A lie she could be lyin. Look! Me swear her eye dem a trimble. Watch her, watch her now. People eatin di food, eatin! How can you eat wid dat filth in front of you. Me no know why di coffin not "Y"-shape, mek me tell you. Too much cocky track in she! God forgive me mout. Me hear seh even on di mainland everybody know bout she – one of di most well known Lampis ever. From when me did firs see her twitching she tail wid di odda Lampis roun town, me know dat she was trouble.

"We can only hope dat in her last moments she found di Lord."

… Hear dem a mek noise outside. Drinkin, laughin. Ungodly. What's wrong wid dem ole whore fren of hers? Me know Glory didn't invite dem! Dey want to drown out the word of di Lord. Glory bes be careful, dem woman deh, dem Lampis – evil! Evil as di day long. Killas dem. Whores, ole higue, all ah dem, witches wid hearts as black as dem face. Dat is really where di bitch in di coffin belong. Wid dem. Dutty heathen!

Look at me chile, watch him nuh! Him ah do me proud, til me heart goin burs! Show di heathens how it go. Show dem, show dem! Praise God di day you come to me. I know him feel bad; dat will soon pass. It did before. Him wife seh she catch him in dat ole bitch house. Being a man of di Lord him shoulda know betta, should not be fraternising wid dese people, but him won't lissen. You would tink dat di Lord woulda give him di strent to resist, to see di devil in all him guises. Is a shame. Is him heart, as big as di open sea out yonder. But is shame, is shame his wife catch him under di house. Dat is where him use to hide when him a pickney. Is him sof nature, jus like him modder. But dat ole whore? She ent have no shame. Still a tek man to her bed at she age. Maybe dat is what kill her; she screw sheself to death. She a burn in di fiery depths of hell. Praise Jesus!

Glory look so sad, cyant look at her, cyant let her catch me eye. She should be glad. I am. God forgive me. Now maybe every god-blessed husband in dis place will be where dem suppose to be. She was di reason mine lef me, I swear pan me pickney life it was. Dat ole hussy bruk up many a marriage on dis island. Man fool so still. Chupid. She come along wid crocodile eyes, tail twitchin, an man tink woman mus be like dat all di time. Glory – likkle, quiet, yellow child. Now, she's a funny woman. Quiet, quiet, not like she modder. I used to see her sometimes, waiting outside di shops or in town. Never smilin. Me memba seeing her outside a shop, sad eyes, playin in di dirt wid a stick. She look so small an helpless, so in need a God, me want hold she, look after she, give she everything that ole whore could not, show her di light. But she fine di Lord an mek him she only judge, praise Jesus. Glory goin need all she strength today.

And look Mikey, dat ole fool cryin in he rum. Him a fool fi she, long years. He bring down him family. He was di only one a dem educate, an him turn fishaman. Imagine dat. Ah she, she bring him dung to her level. She bring we all down.

"Good marnin, good afternoon and goodnight. Hehe, well, we are here, dat is for sure. Hehe. I wanted to seh… Clementina, stop pullin me! She don't want me mek ah fool of myself. Anyway, mek me seh… Is good to… ahm, well dat's it, I'll sit down now."

"Yuh ole fool, yuh did mek a fool of yuself. You come here to mek speech? Like di shame is not enough, Jesus God!"

"Sshh. My love, people will hear you."

"Don't shush me! Why *are* we here, Alfredo?"

"Sweetheart, darlin, sugar, it was, well, ahm, di right ting to do."

"Right? Right?"

"Sweetheart, you didn't have to come."

"Of course I did! What you tek me for? I remember di times, Alfredo, cryin in me marriage bed, knowin where you was goin!"

"Baby…"

"Don't baby me! Do not speak to me as if I was one of you whores! My poor parents, if dey only knew you was goin bring me so low."

"Darling, please, you go antagonise yuhself."

"Oh Holy Sweet Baby Jesus! We in di dead house, at di whore funeral! If you let anyone ah dem duppies follow we home to kill we in our beds cos you needed to come to dis whore funeral! Oh Lord, sweet lord, sweet baby Jesus!"

"Well it didn't seem right not to come. Stop cryin, Clemmy, sweetheart, sugar, darling."

"Alfredo, after everything you said. Look at our little post office. Do you know how many people would kill for what we have? What for do yuh want to throw it away?"

"But darlin..."

"Don't darlin me! Comin home with her smell on you lips an her soul in you heart. Jesus Lord! Di depravity, di sickness. Is a miracle dat we have what we have, Alfredo. A shop, a post office, a house. Dem people would tink nothin of taking away all a dis. Why would you put it all at risk?"

"What dem doin? Peekin tru we windows?"

"Do not bring up you depravity in me face. Shame, Alfredo, have you no shame?"

"I just wanted to pay me respecs..."

"Respecs! Respecs! You tink such as she deserves respec, an you God-given wife none?"

"No, sweetheart."

"Den what?"

"Well, ahm... ahm... I would tink dat God would be pleased wid me, dat me was doin di right ting to... ahm..."

"Check she dead?"

"Exact. You know what dem say bout she and dis family?"

"Alfredo, how strong you tink me modder is?"

"Wha?"

"Me seh, how strong you tink she is?"

"Well... ahm... me no know."

"Is how you tink me come out a me modder as if me born dis size? She would be dead. Well she not dead, Alfredo, an me not born yesterday."

"Alright, alright, but what is di worry?"

"Di worry, di worry, what about di priest, di farders?"

"What, sugar?"

"Di farders. What would dey say, what if our church found out? Aren't you feared for you soul, Alfredo? We have good standing here. Our little post office. It is everyting me modder an farder work for. And one day, twenty years ago, you roll in there like one a di saints almighty and you talked dem to give me to you, me an di post office. You owe me an dem."

"And neither you nor dem go mek me forget it."

"Is what you seh, Alfredo?"

"Nuttin, darling."

"You always savin people? Don't it?"

"I... I... what you mean?"

"Me hear say, Alfredo, me hear say. And you know di mail inspector is comin today, an we haven't got di mail."

"I go pick it up on our way home. What for I have anyting to do wid di inspector?"

"Well he like everyting shipshape an he will be reportin dat we're not in di shop."

"What madness has taken over di worl when a man cyant come to a funeral? Well, me tink seh we set free."

"Why you shoutin, Alfredo? People go hear."

"Let dem hear, Clementina. Dem always hear, wherever we are, dem hear. Whateva we do, dem hear; you cyant poop an smady don't hear!"

"Alfredo! Calm yuself!"

"Well, dem too blasted nosey. I'm goin outside."

"Alright, me a come too."

"Wha!"

"For you to go outside an drink wid dem ole whores – you drinkin buddy and sex fren? You mad! I'm not letting you outta me sight. For people to laugh at me? You lucky me here. Nobody can tell me me nuh know where me husband is. Shut you mout, Alfredo, you'll catch flies. Dat's right. Me a come. Get my hat an shawl."

"But darlin..."

"Hush you lip, Alfredo and let we go outside."

"Is di man me want to talk wid."

"Oh, I see, relive di ole times? Laugh at you dirty ways?"

"Clementina, stay in here wid the ladies. What people tink? You out there wid di man dem and di Lampis, eh?"

"Maybe you have a point, but..."

"Yes, dumpling, you know me right. Stay here, in the kitchen. Glory has made some tea."

"Don't go into that room, Alfredo!"

"What is wrong wid you, Clementina? Di woman dead. You tink she goin to seduce me from di grave?"

"A you talk it Alfredo, a you talk it."

Clementina and Hyacinth

"Miss Hyacinth, you are much in contemplation?"

"Oh, scuse, scuse, Miss Clementina, it is di day, y'know. Death comes to us all and mek you tink."

"Truth is truth and it don't help di holy contemplation, when a noise..."

"Of di devil himself!"

"...is ragin on outside."

"Brazen!"

"Me wonder if dem not fraid?"

"Dem! Dey know nothing of Godly fear, Miss Clementina."

"Yes..."

"An a lot of people who should know better."

"Ahem. When we hear the news, I did not know that she would go down so quick."

"Di devil can't wait to claim him own."

"In truth, Miss Hyacinth, I didn't know what to expect today. Me know she have children, but is it only di one, Glory? Wasn't dere a boy? Wasn't he lost or sumting?"

"I was jus thinkin bout dat. Me surprise she didn't breed up, breed up. But dem seh some people know di ole ways to stop demselves from bearing a child. No true?"

"Me hear dat also. You think she do dat?"

"Nuh mus! She must have juju di seed dem – oh scuse, me mout run weh!"

"Oh, Miss Hyacinth, please! The things you say! Do you really tink so?"

"Yes."

"Er, yes, um, me hear dat."

"Mek me tell you, me tink she kill di boy."

"Wah!"

"Yes! You cyant jus lose pickney like dat. Nobody know what happen to him. Jus one day we hear seh him gone. Dem seh you lose what you don't deserve."

"Not everyone..."

"...is God bless. He don't bless di wicked wid di gift of life. Is not so, Miss Clementina?"

"I... I..."

"Dat crazy granchild she have ent here and needa is the grandson; no one has seen him for years."

"D'you think he'll come?"

"I wouldn't if I was him. Him get weh from dis place. Why would him want to come back?"

"To pay his respects"

"Dat ting deserve respec?"

Mikey

"Unaccustom as I and I is to talking out in public, I want fi say jus a few tings as Jah watches over all a we. I and I soon to tek me leave – no, no, me no mean me goin dead, too, doh me tink some ah you did tink so. Me choose life. I and I is a livin man; me no bargin wid death, no heng roun it, no let it be part of me life. So, me nah stay long, me ah go back up di mountain to me home, where Jah provide, but me feel it important dat someone talk dat knew her long, an I and I will tell you what dis woman mean to me. You all know di I. You all know she was de moon to me sun, di land to me water. Even when me a travel she close to me heart.

"Me nah fraid talk it, feel it. Di young people dem nuh know how to deal with what is in dem heart, but if you don't say what in you heart, you heart goin trangle you. Mark me. Me know what me a talk. Me a talk bout di muscle string, di neck back, di shoulder blade, di han miggle, di foot bottom, di hair up di nose, di eye teet. An das all dat lay dung deh, inna di box, for we know she gone. Dat is just di ting dat use fi house her. All a we haffi tink on dat. We come to we own judgment.

"When me firs see dis likkle ting by di Lampi shed, me know di most high have provide me wid me queen. She tink she too nice. Is how high she nose coulda reach di sky, an she shorter dan we, eh? She start fi work dere, an every day me fine some excuse to go dere. Me start fi put me boat dere, me start fi sell me catch to di Lampi dem, but truly it was so I and I could catch a sight of she. She coulda run up an dung dem steps, up an dung, and when she done she sit down on the rocks and smoke she pipe. She start chat to we. She tell me she name, where she from. Everyting. Dere was no secrets. Me tell her everyting and dat was dat.

Everyting set in stone. It already written. When she want me to teach she how to fish, me tink dat is why she chat to me in di firs place. She didn't know how to swim, growing up here, and she didn't know nuttin about fishin. Me tek she in me boat. She fraid. Yes me know she act like she ent fraid a nuttin, but mek me tell you, she fraid a water, like puss. She sit in di boat stiff so. Scared fi rock it. She seh me is rocking it fi joke and dat when she come back to land she goin stab me! Ha! She soon fine her sea leg. She put her line in and start to fish. Not long after, sumtin grab she line an she start fight. 'Come here, you dutty, stinking was-not fish,' she seh. 'One a we a going end up in di pot tonight!' Ever since den, before me put down my lines, dat is what me always seh, 'One a we goin end up di pot tonight.'

"She and my mother – well some a you will memba me modder. Dat was a battle royal over I, and well, me modder didn't like my involvement wid Sed. She hate fi accept me choice. But yuh have to accept yuh blood. Dat is for sure. If you lucky enough fi have pickney. We not so blessed and some dat are don't deserve it. Yes, and I and I know di troot of it. Anyway. We not here fi dat. We here fi she. So hol up you glass and wish my queen safe journeys."

...I an I tink she did know she soon dead. When me went fi see her di las time, she lay down. She neva git up again. She look at I and I and tell me to lay down nex her. Me fraid.

"You want me inna you bed?" Me shock.

"So?" She had dat look on her face, like you an di worl beneath her. But dat look would tek hol ah me, like bein drawn by you navel string.

"Well it's been a lotta years. You a feel sick fi true."

"You always haffi mash everyting up."

"Alright cool down, sekkle. You mout goin give I and I headache."

"God bless me days. You always sick. You foot, you han', you head. Dis a hurt, dat a twis' arf. Sumting always do you. It like dealin wid a likkle ole woman, to rarse."

"An is yuh mek I and I tek sick, Jah know."

She did know what I mean.

"When you did los di bwoy." A tear run dung me cheek. Pain is still pain.

"Ole man, you no done barl? Dat a fifty years ago."

"Me neva done barl. Neva. But Jah teach we forgiveness an conciliation."

"Is what you talking, ole man? You like dem idiot pan di street."

"A who dat?"

"Dem man, no wash, no comb dem hair, act like dem jus bush people."

"You figet we all bush people. You figet bout you family a bush people an all what dem do? Woman, know thy self."

She stop den, look out yonder window, searchin, me tink.

"You no haffi remine me bout me history, ole man; no one haffi do dat."

"Jah know..."

"Jah know, Jah know. Seem like everybody a catch religion."

"Depend on di religion yuh a catch."

"Dem all di same."

"No sah. Babylon try fi keep we under an use dem religion."

"Yet you an you unwash breddas use di same book backra use fi oppress we. You too contrary to backside, ole man."

"Yuh language bad terrible. Yuh no know how ole you is? Carry yuhself wid some pride, African sister."

"Oh God, me is me, ole man, an you an no odda crab-louse goin change dat."

"I an I done fight wid you. Is dat what you call me for? Lissen to your words dat does hurt I an I ears?"

"I an I, I an I. You soun so fool fool. Come here before me shot you a lick you poop til nex week."

"Not comin near you, man. Sometime man haffi be man."

"By sayin no to me?"

"Dat's right."

"When truly, you nuh want fi say no to me."

"Sometime you haffi do sumting you no like to do. Yuh sick, yuh sen di gyal fi me? What yuh want? I an I have plenty fi do."

"What yuh a do?"

"I goin on a journey, a long way away."

"Wait, you come here fi give me joke?"

An she laugh, dat bad-mine laugh an clap she han on top a di bed.

"Laugh all you want to laugh. Yes, woman, a call has come fi help di Etiopian broddas an sistas an babies slaughter under di tanks of di oppressor."

"But wha we know bout dem? What about we?"

"We all di same, don't you know dat? We mus know each an every one of us is di same or we perish. So say me kith an kin over di wata."

"Not dat jackass dat want all ah we fi go back to Africa?"

"Him is di prophet most high."

"Him! Me did know him uncle; yuh neva saw a man so tief."

"Sed!"

"An what good did it do you di las time?"

"Dat was a long time ago. Maybe now di time is right."

"You pick up you foot, seh you goin fight di war a di righteous, pan an island dat have no relation to we, an what happen? We free?"

"I an I was young den."

"An you ole now. Look pan you, you can hardly walk. You can barely liff up youself. Look how you back ben'. Look how you foot stan when you came back before. Is me nurse you. Maybe me won't be here to nurse you dis time."

An she let di words drop an pitch outside. She did know.

She always try to catch me dat way. Always use death against me. Even my own. Di way a man know death different from a woman. I look dung at dese hands, dem have di tremble in dem dat get worse by di day. Bwoy, but ole age cruel. Maybe I an I cyant fight no more, is words now dat me haffi deal wid, not gun an knife.

Me look up an see dat she know me mine.

"Is whe you a go? You lef sumting out dere?"

Me know now what she a talk. After all dese years it still a get to she. Suddenly me feel betta bout getting ole cos di ole fowl still a feel jealous.

"Always a talk bout fight! Which part you can fight now. Can hardly tan up straight."

"Is war out dere, Sed." Me point out di window, the window she use to survey she queendom, she subjects – she keep she eye pan everyting in Paradise an beyond.

"Is a war in here to blood-eye, a war in here. Always war. People talk nex war a come."

"I an I tell you."

"An when it done, Church here still. An you can come home in a box, if dem fine you pieces. Lissen, ole man. Can you stop di trimble in you han an see straight nuff fi fire di gun?"

"I an I know all bout gun."

"You sure you not goin shoot youself inna yuh one good foot?"

"No tell me bout gun, me can still fire a gun."

"Den come fire it fi me, nuh?"

"No."

So many times I see her on a wooden cot covered wid rags, in her hut on di alley, pon the sand, against a tree, under di stars, in di warm sea, pon a rock by di river, in di cole river. Layin dere, waitin fi me. Brown legs open, black eyes shut. Me no tink seh she know she did love me, but di look dat live in she eye dat day tell me she did feel it. And, of course, she right. Who was I? Ole man. But who we is if we stop fight?

"Come here, nuh."

"No."

"You no want to love me before you go?" She teasin me, she did know dat me not goin nowhere.

"We both too ole fi dat."

"So you mean you not too ole fi fight, an limp up an dung inna a foreign, an get you tail shoot off, but you too ole fi love. Man brain tun backward."

"No."

"You piece a shit."

"You see it. You no like people fi tell you no. I might be ole, an a shek, an have bad foot an han but today me a tell you no."

"You wah?"

"You hear me. All dese years, you want dis, you want dat, you say jump, me mussa seh how high? Is a miracle I and I not dead arready."

"No worry bout dat, ole bumbo, you time soon come."

Jah knows dat woman could mek me mad. But me feet did carry me forward, like dem know what me don't. Den she grabbed me hans an put dem all over her. I an I shock. Me heart not so good no more, an from time to time me foot swell up. But by di time me get me clothes off an fol' dem up, me have to wake she up. Me cyant believe it.

"Sed, me no know if me heart can tek it."

"You damn arse, what wrong wid you?"

"Me mean it, Sed, me heart bad."

"You heart bad like me backside. You wortless ole dutty rastaman."

"But Loo sen fi me, seh yuh sick, an yuh a carry on in dis way?"

"What kin' a rarse you a talk, bwoy?"

"I and I is older dan you; is who you a call bwoy?"

"Come nuh, man, me nuh have all day. You nuh see seh one of us soon dead."

Dat woman mout was bad. An' dat is how we stay di whole afternoon. Was like ole times. We both a we put on a likkle weight, but if we hold in we bellies and tek it slow we manage. After all dese years, me know she body betta dan me own. She use she legs to prop me up. Me struggle to fine her. She try to guide me but it mek her muscle contrac, an me neck get crick. Heh heh, yuh never know seh hundred-year-olds can still carry on so, eh. Den di strangest ting happen. Sed start fi cry. She wasn't barling. Dat was not her way, just a likkle tear follow her cheek down and res pan di pillow. Cryin is nuttin to me. I and I barl fi no reason all di time. I could be doin' anyting – readin di paper, sleepin, shittin, anyting – an me start barl, me no know what for, or what start it, but di tears come. I and I feel is Jah passin over. No, di strangest ting was dat she let me put me arms roun her. She let me comfort her. Me couldn't be more shock if someone come up to me in di rum shack an seh me is di king a Inglan. She hold I and I face. Believe me to Jah, I saw dis day.

...She look good today. Glory do she hair. Di floor is wet wid how people dash down dere drink for her. Me do di same. One fi she, one fi I and I.

Glory

"Tank you all for coming. I know Momma would be pleased to see you all here. For some of you it is di firs time you in our house. It gives me pleasure to welcome so many friends here, to help bury me modder, pay her respect. She work hard, hard, hard, an some of you would know dat at firs hand, but she did work all of her life and when in dese las years, she tek to her bed, she still had sumting to say, advice to give, knowledge to share. Her love was without bounds.

"She was a good provider, she taught me the ways of the world. She loved her grandchildren, always ready wid a joke and a shiny penny. She will be missed, she will be missed. I am so, so pleased to see you all come to pay you respects..."

... I know she here... can feel she eyes lookin from behind di closed lids. Well, me know, she won't be here long. She must've start her journey, long time – we all do. Some say we start dat journey from birth. I believe dat. I did my best. Only God know what kind a woman she was; what kinda a modder, only I knew. I thought I would see her, thought she would come to me, but maybe she decide me not worthy. I never was. Never was. Di duppy dem dat live in dis house use to be me only company. Me only friend inna di worl. No decent somebody would be me fren. No one would let dem chile come to di whore's house. Me have to build meself up, start from di bottom – so low dat earth nearly cover me, so low dat me can't see no sun, for it block out. Dat is how me start me piece a life, in Paradise.

She use to put me to bed when me hungry. Yes, I was hungry

many times. You tink her body feed us, make us rich? No, we stay poor, from when I was a child through to woman. Poor. Is me bring us up. Me. Me modder didn't know no other way to be. She get use to thinkin on she back. Dere were times when nobody want her, nobody want pay for her. We still at Paradise Alley. We collect rain water in a barrel out di back. Seduce learn to fish. She take Mikey boat and go out sheself, always at night when di fish sleepin. Still eating dat same likkle fish day after day was enough to put you off fi life. When any a di Lampis really hungry, dem would bring a likkle pan an tek home di renk fish dem jus done spice an cook. Dat is when you know dat woman was findin tings hard. When you could smell it coming out she house, stinkin up di whole yard. And when an islan man smell it, him not coming near you, but di others, di whites an di odda people from all over, dem love it. It got so dem tink di lampi smell was actually di woman – dat is how dey come fi share di same name.

An every now an den Seduce get sick. High fever, shakin. Sometime she did talk foolishness. All a di Lampis get it one time or another. Wid Seduce it was always fever. Some a dem turn funny colour, some a dem broke out in a sore all over dem body, den dey would have to wash in a special bush bath and wait. Dey swear it was di sailors give it to dem. She would have to stay in bed all day. Di odda Lampis would come round wid a bit of soup or sumting. Sometime, early morning when moon an sun share the sky, dem singing would wake me up. A humming dat got louder and louder. Like di noise dem a mek outside now. What dem goin to achieve? She's not coming back an she ent getting into heaven.

..."Marmee, me hungry."

"What's dat?"

"Me hungry."

"Alright, alright, come." I would climb into bed next her and we'd both pretend to fall asleep.

When she sick was di only time she love me, di only time she let me near her. I remember one night. I was cryin nex to her, me belly burnin. She jump up and me tink she was goin to fish. Only later, when I was waitin for her, did me see di net Mikey mek for us still in di corner. She come back, wash herself, put the bread an a small pot a soup on di table, an turn roun an get back into bed.

She tell me bout me farder. He was a sailor. An almost white black man. From di mainland. Him name Washington. She name me after di ship that bring him. Me modder say she chose him for me, to mek my life betta dan hers. Dat is why she neva like me husban, cos him black, blacker dan anyting me ever see. Even in me mid thirties, I still tryin to upset her, an upset her me did. She tell me him black, black like poison. A poison headin straight for she heart. I knew dis, for it was me dat choose di poison and watch it move to its final restin place. She knew he was taking me away. When me come back widout him she neva ask what happen, where he was. I think she always knew. We jus carry on as if I neva left.

She use to pretend she dead. She'd be talkin and den next minute she on the floor, still, not movin, eyes wider dan open. I'd run to her, throw me small arms roun she neck, tears about to come. Then she'd grab me, hug me up an laugh an laugh, and den say, "You love me?"

"Yes, Mama."

"You mean it?"

"Yes, Mama."

She always act like she do me di favour of givin birth to me. I'd get up and go into di yard, feelin disgusted with her, but not knowing why. Feelin used, put upon. She really dead now, fi true. She can't get up and laugh and laugh and make me feel disgusted. Laugh how she force all these people here if she was just playin again? When man came into di house, I use to want her to play dead then, but she neva did.

What she couldn't stand was that I could see things she couldn't see. One day me feel a box cross my face before me know what it was. Likkle points of light flash round me. I fell in love wid di sparks an didn't want dem to fade. Then me see she confuse eyes staring down at me.

"Is yuh chat to yuhself like you blasted mad? You grandmodder mad, you know, mad as ole arse. You want follow?"

She box me again, but dis time my face numb, me didn't feel a thing. Me tryin to keep di lights wid me.

"Me seh is wah you a do?"

She drew me up from the kitchen floor, dis kitchen floor. She look in me eye. We'd only been in dis house a few days. I was eight. She shook me.

"Is what you a do?"

I glance over at di ole lady wid flowers growin out her nose. She put a finger to her lips and slowly disappear. Sed glance backwards and den look at me.

"Is what dere?"

My mouth open and close, open again but the words get stuck. The outline of the ole lady still there, but fadin. She seem to be turnin an talkin to someone. Sed couldn't see her and she knew it. This mek her even more angry and she dash me to the ground and start runnin around from room to room, cussing like di whore she was.

"You dutty, nasty, bumboclart you! You devils, you wotless pieces of shit, you no good, no use, dead as anyting. Go back to you modder cratches. Me ah go dash piss pan you! You pussyclart. May Jesus tear you limb from limb. You fucking rarse hole you!"

She was trying to get rid of whoever she couldn't see. Duppy no like swearing; it offend dem. She was trying to frighten dem into leaving. It didn't work.

Me nuh like di dress she get to wear. Pastor Collins' wife bring it. A strange dress with flowing sleeves that seem to glint in the light, the colours of a peacock, like the feather in Uncle Alfredo hat. Me nuh tink dat Mumma woulda like it. But at least it look a modest dress for a ole whore.

..."Me time a come."

"Yes, Mama."

The last time me saw her alive I was straightening tings in her room. I jus tell we helper fi sweep it out.

"No, no Glory, no sweep now, di dus sekkle pan me ches."

"But it have to do, it will mek you ches feel betta. Come, Daphine, come."

Daphine hesitate. She no like to do anyting fi upset di ole woman, but is me pay she wages.

"I seh come, Daphine."

"Me not long fi here." She been sayin dis for di past four years, since she took to her bed one day an neva come out.

"Yes, Mama."

"Me soon give up. Ent nuttin worth di fight."

"Yes, Mama."

"You tell Son?"

"I write him las month. I tell you."

"Him comin?"

"I don't know."

"Where me grandarta?"

"Somewhere." I didn't know. I still don't know.

Daphine stop sweeping a moment, an den carry on. Mama cough.

"Rahtid, you a try fi kill me?"

I left the room, not wanting to hear her profanity, praise God. She always do that – mek every God ting my fault. Loo is me chile, ent nuttin can change dat, but it was Mumma dat trouble di gyal wid all kinda foolishness, tell she bout di legend of Lucretia, an how she a slave from Africa, an how she free herself wid poison an hide out in the mountains. I go always blame Mama for confusin me chile's mind, so she start speak fi she *an* fi Lucretia. Me not know nutten bout Lucretia. Me know me not relate to any African. My past is di Lord, not some African criminal. Dat is why I call her so, to show everybody me not fraid a di ole gossip.

When me went back wid her soup she gaspin for breath, her eyes half closed. She hold out her hand. I could not touch it but instead stroke her head an call Daphine.

Me don't tink di goat is enough fi feed everybody. Is how dem all a come wid dem long bellies? Before dis, nobody want us in dem house, an if dem did, we eat before we left we house.

Don't eat from people. No sir. It's been a long time since we been together.

...What a way dat white-haired mongrel pastor a chat an mix up wid people! Like him belong! Jus cos him tink he fine di Lord, don't mean Him fine you. Lord forgive me, but me heart cyant hold him. Had to bring him, true, is what Seduce would want, but having him back in my house fill me wid sumtin me cyant explain. Don't go to his church. Cyant tek it – too quiet. Me need to find God wid me voice, to celebrate His name, to know God is vengeful, dat di wicked get punish, not forgiven. What is di point of that? Me not Hyacinth, but evil mus be punish.

Why Son not here? I send word to him, sayin dat he should know she goin down. Him know him have to be here. If she call, you have to answer, but me really don't know if him goin come.

But after di funeral – if him turn up – Son mus go back to mainland, where it's safe for him. Safe for men. If him stay is putting him life at risk. Men don't do so well in dis family, but he know. Maybe he already on a boat when she closin her eyes? Maybe when she draw she las breath, he at the quay, waitin for taxi to pull him back up the hill, up to us? Me know she call him, she stretch over water an time an earth an body and call him and he mussa hear her, for all him education an such, he mussa hear her. More than he hears me. She want Son to see her leave dis earth.

Loo tek off as soon as people come.

"Pastor, if you would be so... kind as to... start?"

Daag. I hope he's quick.

"Yes, preacha man, come yuh rarse, you!"

"Tell us what we done know."

"Wooiii!"

"Ah sweat dem ah sweat dem fear, but we alright."

"Nah do nuttin to dem yet."

"Let the banyan tree hold di soun a we voice."

"Let the banyan tree carry di soun a we voice."

"Let the banyan tree spread di soun a we voice."

"To us, to we finga an toe an all in between, to Lampi and Lampi life."

"To Lampi life an Lampi death."

"To di biggest Lampi of dem all."

"Heh hey!"

"Keep di rum coming yah, we here all night."

"True."

"She mus be cussing blue murder right dere, right now."

"A true dem no care."

"True."

"Watch di preacha nuh!"

"Bastard of di bush, him ah fight it, but is where we go, is where all ah we go or all hell pop today."

"Sad fool, him best not stand in we way."

"No one betta stand in we way or blood will run."

"Like virgin pan she weddin night."

"Like chicken on feast day."

"Like di blood of birthin."

"No one can tes we."

"Look at de holy roller she sen fi push her poor modder into di groun, to push an keep pushin."

"Heh, you know how church man stay."

"No, but me tek a lot a dem money inna me time."
"Heh hey!"
"Dem cyant stop we."
"She woulda a hate dis. All dis. But today pickney nuh have no respect."
"True."
"Figet di old ways."
"No worry, Sed, we not leaving you."
"To Seduce!"
"Dem tink we no know dem come fi bury her. We come fi release her, y'hear?"
"People nuh see we?"
"Dem see we, dem fraid."
"A wha?"
"A wha we know."
"True."
"But Sed would want us here."
"Duties to perform."
"Is alright, dem know."
"Stir up di pot deh, sistah, me mout a wait fi di likkle food!"
"She mus a cuss dem now."
"What dese people a do here, what dem want?"
"Free food an entertainment."
"True."
"Dese young ones, no respec."
"You seh dat already, Miss May."
"Wha?"
"You seh dat already."
"Not fi di ole ways."
"Yes Miss May, yuh done talk."
"Lef her, she a reason."
"Me no want to go inside dere, y'know!"
"No, me needa."
"Not me, no sah."
"Dem mus wan fi check she dead."
"True."
"But she live an she dead, an dat is dat."
"Keh, kay ya, look pan dem."

"Look pan di clothes."
"How much cocky you mus get troo fi dat deh money!"
"Only di one you need, di right one."
"Is who yuh a look pan?"
"Yes Mrs Lady, a yuh we a talk."
"Stir up di pot."
"Pass di rum, ya."
"Galang gyal, you time done, you mus go to come back."
"No, she a hang on."
"Not long now, not long."
"Go res yuself, go res."
"No worry yuself, we will tek yuh, we will tek yuh."
"Yuh wan help, Missy? Galang den, tek you dry foot inna di house."
"Yuh don't belong out yah."
"Yuh want help, Missy? Me can wash, sew, cook, whatever Missy want... Cho! Move yuself, let di john crow pick arf you bones. Yuh ah walk but yuh dead long time."
"Long time."
"Dese uppity browns act like di blood dat run troo my vein don't run troo dem vein dem."
"True."
"You want maid, Missy... What you mean? Galang before me cut yuh troat. You hear wha she seh bout me is tief? Tief you husband las night. Yuh not white, yuh know."
"Guweh, yuh favour baboon backside."
"Dem red bitches bring us all down."
"Like dem nuh haffi wipe dem arse."
"Yuh not like dem, Jacqueline, yuh is one of us."
"True."
"Dat's right."
"But dem? Larks man, dem give we pain."
"Not long now, not long."
"No worry yuself, Sed, we not leaving you to dese figet-bouts, no know bout dem culture or ancestors or di ole ways. We will tek you, we not leaving you to dem."
"Wata wash wata, wata wash wata, wind blow breeze. We will do what needs to be done."

"Stan up, holy roller."
"Rock and find you god, Pastor Collins."
"Sweat you praises, holy roller."
"You tink dat will get you to where you need fi go?"
"Di ones dat shout di loudest..."
"Are truly di hemptiest."
"Mek dem know you."
"We surprise you come back."
"Didn't you god try fi stop you?"
"Jackarse!"
"Los' boy."
"But me nuh know who him favour."
"Him favour him longin."
"Hiii! Is true!"
"Stan strong, holy roller."
"Come wid it, holy man."
"If anyting like dat breathes!"
"Not much longer fi you now."
"Only the sea know she true name."
"And keep it to sheself..."
"In the blue-black waters and rocks and in the birds and crabs dat nest dere."
"Come, we wait."
"She waits."

Pastor Collins

"We have gathered here today not to praise her but to bury her. We have come here today not to say goodbye but say praise be, for we will be seein her again in the light of the Lord. We have come here today to give thanks, not cry and be sad at her passin but to remember her with fondness, with grace an forgiveness in our hearts. She is gone but never will be forgotten.

"Let me firs say a thank you to Brother Ceefus for letting me partake of this funeral, although I know some of you prefer the hell and damnation of that church rather than love and understandin. As I understand it, it was at the behest of my godmother. For that is how I saw her, a mother with God. It's a shame we're not in your fine church, Brother Ceefus, but I understand the roof is being repaired. Isn't that so, Brother? My own church is not far, but Sister Glory said that Mother Sed would've wanted it here. Where she was born, where she grew up, where she died.

"The other thing is to let you all know that Brother Brown's funeral will take place next Sunday. So we shall all be together again. There will be hell to pay if I find out that poor Brodder Brown was snatched from us in di prime of his life, because some misguided soul put their faith in the bush teas an rituals prescribe by heathens. You know who you are. Surely his death proves such superstitious practices don't work. They may even have killed him. Stop it and fear di anger of the Lord.

"Now to the business at hand. For many years there have been unfounded rumours about dis house. Even on di mainland, where I lived for many years, people told tales about it. Well, I used to come to this house often many years ago, and again when I came back from my studies wid me wife in tow and been back here many times since, and I never seen a thing, duppy or anyting else. I thank those of you who have overcome such heathen fears and decided to come today. While our late sister never came to church, she always believe in a higher power and it is dat power that has brought us all here today.

"Now I know dat many here feel Mother Sed coulda lived her life better, coulda been a better person, but those who live inna glass shack, let dem trow di first stone. But we must be careful, broddas and sistas, we must be vigilant, for di devil is never far away. We must be on our guard for di evil, di bad mind, di green-eye devil dat snaps at all we heel. Keep Jesus in your heart, close to your soul. You can't worship Him with you body, you can't worship Him wid money; you give Him you life, as He gave his for you. Amen.

"I remember when me an me wife firs come to dis parish. Dis being my first one, many of you felt I was too young an inexperience to do di Lord's work. Di first one to put she faith in me was di lady we passin today. Yes, she took us into her home, she gave us so much warmth an light dat di Almighty decide dat Him did need dat light close to him. He need her for Himself. He had sumting else for her to do. When I came back, she made us welcome, she extended di han of friendship an even deliver my first born. To me she was our eyes an ears, she was our heart an soul, she was our conscience. She made you look within yourself and question your own deeds. Now I'm not here to wash out me mout pan anybody, I'm just here to say dat di Almighty forgives all sins, di Almighty is love an togetherness. And who are we to judge, who are we? In dat spirit, let me ask dat you do not go into di bush, dat you ignore our lost sisters outside, dat you do not partake of di old heathen practices dat we have fought so hard to rid dis parish of. Let us remember di one true God an conduct ourselves in His mercy. You would be laughin in His face if you decide dat you need to commune wid those forces of evil you think is di spirit of this island. We do not need to sing those songs, chant those words, beat those drums, do those pagan dances dat is so close to the devil. I hear a rumour dat a few people tink it alright to cut up animals in barbaric sacrifice in order to free her soul. I'm here to tell you dat her soul is already free an wid di Lord, as we are standing here.

"For the Lord says, Come as you are, come as you are, come as you are. Flesh will not get into heaven. Sin will not get into heaven. Bangarang noise an drum will not get into heaven. Praise di Lord, praise di Lord, praise di Lord. Sing his name. I'm not here to get her into heaven or hell. I am not her judge, I am not her judge. Are you? There is room for all in my father's house, you hear, dere is room in my father's house, praise di Lord. In my father's house all are welcome.

"Let me take advantage of so many people gathered today and just get a bit of town's business out of the way. There is a lot of speculation about di future right now. We cannot hope to know, only God Almighty knows, but I do know there will be no war, so I urge some of di young men, eager to leave us, full of blood lust, to think again. Many of you have already lived through great wars and are understandably anxious. No one has the desire to see those times again, no one wants death and destruction. And whilst the gossip is rife on the mainland, we can be assured on this little piece of God's creation, Church Island, dat we have more sense... Follow me in prayer and in doin so, perhaps, we can reflect on the life of this woman..."

Seduce

Mark me, mark me, me cyant move til what me have to tell is told, till what me have to do is done, like di sun haffi bow before di moon each day and lissen to the stars being dash out, one by one, one by one.

I fuckin hear dem. Di men. Laughin, drinkin, jokin an a carry on so. An me? Lying here, jus dead. I can still hear dem a chat bout di women dem love an chat bout dem wife, dem pickney. Hah! Some a dem bitches husbans and farders did well know me. Me hear di sound of sawin, di sound a hammerin and shaping. Men workin wid wood. Dem mekkin up me rarse coffin! I fine a likkle peace inna di soun. I can hear everyting, now. Me can hear what me seh yesiday, as well as me hear me long ago cry fi me momma titty, as well as me hear tings yet to be. Not ready yet, not ready yet, me cyant move til what me have to tell is told, but me soon come.

Can't see who in dis room. Some bumbo did put some water to me lips and it drip down me cheek an roun me neck. Someone try fi scratch out me dry head. It was eeda dat bitch of a daughter or she crazy pickney. Me no know what me do to her. But dat deh ole fowl? She want fi see me inna di groun like everybody else in dis yah place. Wan' fi know me dead. You imagine dat, you own daughter! Well, me hope she happy now. Lord know, me try everyting.

But larks, when it come, it come, nuh true? An you really is on you own, even if you did have a fambly dat love you. Me? Me have dis ya fambly. All a dem fuckers, yah, all a dem.

As me face cool wid di damp rag pat pan me face, it catch a breeze from di window. When was di las time me see dat view, di same me modder look pan, an me granmodder before she? I did see di town, once so likkle an shart, tryin to inch its way up me hill, did see di bay, di hills an mountains movin away from it, and ships an fisherman an di boats wid names like *Precious* an *Darlin* an *Sweet Baby* restin in di swell.

What a ramblin shit hole dis island still is! Me nuh know why it exist, fi what purpose. Poop out di mainland, it just float in its water, like sumtin nasty, infectin people who live, work an die here. Dis just a rock off di main land. Dere is one more bigger dan we – but nobody live dere – an a few smaller. Di ting bout Church is where it stan. For some reason, when di wind reach our shores it jus stop, an go roun us. An it have a nat'ral harbour. In my day, ships couldn't move fi ships inna dat bay. Di sea, as orange as di clouds tekkin light from di travelling sun – is dere di colour green in hell? Oh, to never see di colour green again, di blue-green of mountains, pale green a grass, di dutty green a di sky before big rain, di deep, deep green of a pear leaf, an bright green of di crappo!

A hell me a talk, for dat is where me a go, so people been tellin me all me life. An dat deh yellow hog, dat pitch from me, she seh she fine Jesus, but she still a go to hell, too. Like all di women inna me fambly. We no have no choice. It decide arready.

...When me listen, me hear so many people in me house me can't count dem. Dem jus a jam up in every room. Some mus be di warrin duppy dem, waitin fi me to join dem, tek sides, be wid dem, blasted triumphant, as dem watch my las life's light go out. Dey jussa count down di minutes. Wait nuh, soon come.

What sawing sound am I memberin doh, ee? Me grandma, Big Pearl before Swine, sawin off di branches of di cedar tree herself fi her crazy daughta, or di men dem sawin it down fi me? Now, dere was a woman; she was big, tall, strong like ox, til she pass. Big Pearl call it as she see it, an she see me an cross herself fi di whole ah her days. Women don't mek like she no more. Many people wonda if it's fine she fine me momma, Little Pearl, not birth she. Dem seh she couldn't be more different – small, shy, gentle. She die of a broken pussy. Pussy call out and get no reply, it sufficate di res ah you. Big Pearl bury her sheself, no body help she. She put me fi sit down nex to her – me not walkin yet – as she fill in di grave.

... "You res now," she seh. "You in di bes place, now yuh are wid you farder, don't memba him name, but him a wait fi you. You grandmodder, great grandmodder, dem will look after you, school you in di ways of di Lord. Don't know if you goin to reach heaven, girl, for yuh degradation was great and yuh begat a chile from evil, but yuh no have to scream no longer. Everybody roun here feel relief di screamin stop. Know dat you gone, an walk in peace. I will foreva pray for you."

She a talk an a sing, talk, whisper, sing, talk like Likkle Pearl was answerin back. It come in like she tryin to convince Likkle Pearl she dead. Maybe dat is her, in di corner, eyes silent, watching me, waitin fi me. Will me go to di same place as you, me modda?

Don't even know if me lip a move. Dere is dat damp rag again, wiping me mout, lettin a likkle cool water trickle an fall in. Di men outside a drink to me. Di Lampis, dey waitin. Glory have she church fools mekkin some noise wid dem tambourines an ole-woman high voices. What dem know about me? What Jesus know bout me? Mek dem stan. Di good ladies of Church Island have come to mek sure me pass. Not yet...

Me mout full but silent, me mout full a words but dem don't leave it, like me ancestors before me, condemn to death, to swing on the hanging tree, to fester, til John Crow come and feast on the words still in dem, whatever is left of dem mout.

And let we rememba how we come to Church Island. Is like all di odda islands an like none a dem. Not rebellious like Jamaica, not surrender like Barby, not confuse like Trinidad, not mash up like Guiana, but mash up in him own way, confuse and mash up like no other. We come to Church to live an to die. Paradise fi some, hell fi odders. A halo of cloud surround we, keeping di breath in an out you body, hot an wet, cloud reflecting di land, with hills, mountains, peaks an valleys – dark secret tunnels dat always still moving out yonda when we reach near dem. Is where di mountains connect wid di sky dat di wind gadders di voice of di ole ole an di new new, an run troo trees an fling troo hills an smash troo rock, an raise up di soun, "Hoy! Hoy! Sed get tek in! Hoy!"

Part of Church fall inna di sea, under di weight of di new religion. Religion mash it up. Everybody lose respec for the old ways, figet di ole days, pray fi di now. But new no mean betta, no sah, it only mean what someone else figet. Me memba a man-trap dat point to di fambly buryin groun. Dat was Grandmama Pearl Before Swine who put it dey. When we was set free, dem did dash di manacle an tongue-trap an body-cages into the sea. She seh dem fool, fool. She keep di man-trap right outside dis house. She seh she want to clap she eye pon it every day. To memba di pain. Dem tings of torture, cole hard steel, nails an spikes an traps may be gone, but, to backside, dem still here, in each and every one of us. Not gone yet.

Me use to play pan it as a child, yes. When we move back, me move it from di front to di side a di house. It long, long, long, wid two points at each end to bury inna di groun. An it paint black. In di miggle it look like jaw, like a giant's mout widout skin or muscle, jus teet. A giant open mout waitin in di groun fi snap you in two. Me use to play like it was a carriage, like fi di fancy ladies in town.

An me rememba back to di town call Paradise. Where we wage di war of wars upon each odda, every day climbin on to one anodda backs, like frogs fuckin, but is not pleasure we seekin, is fi crush one anodda an try fi survive. Where di browns an blacks an a few chupid whites fight for a place widdin we own history. We dash out di whites – too rude, too stink, too tief. We show dem Paradise! Oh yes, we know dem still a control tings but not in fimmi eyeline. But we mash dem up good.

And den we come to di house, my backside house, fi me sins, me momma sins and me granmumma sins and for all dat was before and yet to be, we have dis house. Surround by creepin trees, built pon our backs wid our blood, wrestle out di han of an ole quack, who treat every illness wid di same sulphur medicine until him own bloated, crumblin face did dead self. I did tink di house – orange-pink against green land – look like di veins of a cook parrot fish, runnin away from di town creepin up di hill. Is a house where duppy and memories fight fi attention in di dark corners, makin a holy show of demselves. But town catchin up to us, in the way dem always do. What will tek di house first: di town, di duppy dem or di bush?

Soon.

Yes man, when me was young di bay white wid sail. Ships still dock dere but now dem mek outta steel not wood. An di lampi sheds pan di far side, di cramp-up wooden shacks behine dem, where dem buy we flesh, an love was nowhere. Yes, man, di place full a sailors from around di worl an me lay wid all a dem. Dat is how me fine Glory farder.

Me wonder if di man-juice know what it doin? If dem can tell who dem belong to or where dem want fi go? If more dan one man juice inside yuh, does yuh body choose which juice yuh want? Me tink so, me know so.

Me memba when me firs clap eyes pon him. Me spot him pan di boat when I was on di shore, sewin. Sometime di sailors dem want dem clothes mend – it was a way of earnin a likkle sumtin if di coochie not up to it. It was a day when me mine restless, could not quiet, and all of a sudden me realise why, as me watch him come down di gangplank, curly light-brown hair, like a halo, circlin him head. Him walk like him not in control of him arm an legs, dem just go wey dem want. Me wait a long time for dis man. Me body want a child, an I want fi mek sure it get di best start. Me wait. Me know him comin. Him an his friends mek dem way through di town an through di woman. Nobody could tell me nuttin bout him cos me already know all about him. Him easy smile give way dat him use to woman fightin ova him. Me want di right man, an he was right, his body right, an his hazel eyes was right.

"Can you see the butterflies, see how much love they show di tree? What you say, Sed, what you say?"

"I not sayin nuttin, me jus a wait fi yuh."

"How long will you wait?"

Him always ask chupid question. Him always want more from di worl dan what tan inna him pocket.

"Will you miss me?"

Big eyes, big teet, big head, body containing seed dat will spawn mine.

"Miss you what?"

We were on di beach, near the sheds, di sand stick to our bodies and me see the stars reflec in di sweat dat shine on me skin. Star fi star. Me know dat she was growin, me know dat she was comin to be.

"I want you to miss me."

Dem want, dem no want, dem want, want, want.

"Why does what you want have anyting to do wid me?"

"I want you to miss me."

Hidiat. Him already do what him do. Me no need him again.

"I chose you."

Ches high, high, til him cyant see him foot. Jackarse. I chose you.

"I don't get you meanin."

Tek note, all a man want is fi you to look like you ah listen to dem. Dem love dat more dan when dem sex you.

"I coulda been with anyone of those girls, yes ma'am, anyone. Agnes or Lucy, but I chose you."

"So what? You want a trophy cup and colours like you is a winnin horse?"

"Ha! Seriously though, baby, we set sail soon. I will be gone; we will not see each other again."

Dat's right, time to go.

"Did you hear me? We might not see each other again."

"So what you tink? You want me to come to di mainland? Dat shit hole! You wouldn't ketch me dead dere. Or you want to live here wid me? Amongst di sheds and di life?"

"Hell no!"

Me know so. Jus wanted to see how far him would tek di lie.

"I been at sea five years, five years. I need to go home."

"Back to you wife?" Him eyes wide out so, he cover his mouth and smile behind him hand.

"I'm not married." His voice come from far away, not the same as the others. Me could hear meself in it.

"Where you from?"

"From here."

"Oh."

He couldn't believe me was from here. Nobody see Church as any place at all.

"Will you miss me?"

"No."

"You is a bitch. Miss me!"

"No."

He lif me pan his lap, the roughness of the sand still on his fingers.

"You, I'll think bout you forever."

Some men chat too much.

When we firs see him, not only me but di res of di Lampis want him. Mos men nuttin to look at, nuttin to fire you. Mos men dry like grass, dull like old river mud. When a woman fine a pretty man, she might fight fi him. If him pretty an yellow? Fight to di death bruk out. We all want him, but to my mine him already mine and he come from me eye an me heart an me dreams.

"What yuh name?"

"Washington, after the president."

"What you ship call?"

"It's called *The Glory Be*".

"Dat is what our daughta will be called, Glory."

"Oh, you want my seed?"

"Me have it arready."

"So, you want me?"

"No, me have you seed."

"Why me?"

"Because me want me pickney to have a life. Me want her to have what me neva get."

"So you did choose me."

Me jus hope me pickney not as fool as him. She haffi get she brains from me. Lard. Cyant stan a chupid man.

"Maybe I can come back, maybe I can come back for you?"

"You cyant even fine you two foot an han! Is how you goin fine me?"

"You goin to be doin this. I know. Whenever I come back, you goin to be right here. I know it."

"Is how you know?"

"Because you're a whore in your heart. This is where you're supposed to be."

Me tink bout dat, tink bout usin di knife me have strapped to me waist, tink about usin it and tekkin a piece ah him to dash inna di sea. Den me tink, no, what me tell me daughta? Me stab you poopa? Though me sure dat is not di firs time anyone eva say dat.

"You know everyting?"

"No, but I know women like you, all over the world, yes sir. Had them all too."

"And what about you, massa-all-over-di-world. Men like you? Tall and chupid!"

"At least I know my place."

"An what place is dat? Under buckra boot heel?"

"My father was white, my mother was mulatto."

"You mean you farder some nasty bitch dat tek any gyal him want?"

"They were together."

"Is dat so? She have a choice?"

"You don't know anything about it."

"You shame, shame ah youself, hate youself?"

"For what?"

"Fi not bein white?"

Di slap him give me was nuttin and to tell you di troot, me know him was goin to get there. Fool.

Di odda Lampis dem congratulate me. Glory was so very fair an she have good hair. She have to be set for glorious deeds, she future away from Paradise Alley.

Me watch di ship leave, me watch it long time, me climb over di rocks in di harbour an stay an watch an watch. Di sun come down an me still dere. Me want di baby to keep a glimpse of him, knowing me not goin to see him again, an me glad. What fi you want man? What dem do? Tax you, stress you, tek you money, hate you and you children.

Me carry her fi di normal time. Not like me, me grandmodder say. Me modder, she carry me a year. Glory was di normal ten months. Still work but have to do sumtin else odda than wid di man dem. When di pains start, me was up a ladder, mixin di lampi. A ship was in an' waitin. Di pain get me in di back at firs, den move roun. All di women dere was experience midwife an aborters. Dem bring all dem knowledge of all di herb an bush, so me know me would be alright.

When me did have Glory, me want get way from di Alley. But couldn't. Me never happy wid her around. Some Lampi happy for dem to live an die on di Alley, happy for dem children to watch dem live like dat. Me tink dat was wrong. Up until den me never really care bout myself. Den you have a pickney an everyting change. Everyting is fi dem. Some pickney mix up di spice fi di lampi. Some haul di catch from di fisherman boat up to di yard. Me even see some women set dem girlchild to work. Some a dem girlchild disappear on di ships. Was no life. All me could tink bout was getting out of di Alley. Strange, me never tink of goin home to stay before, back to di house on di hill. Di house beautiful, wid di sea in di distance, but it was run down when me livin dere, so before Glory me never go back. Too much memories, too much pain. But me know afta Glory it was time fi go back.

When man come, me use to give Glory to Juicy Lucy next door. When man come to her, she send her pickney dem stay wid me. She have five, all a dem different colours, from pale to dark, dark. Once, me memba, Lucy wasn't in an a man come to me door. Me just finished cookin. Di man was Rigo. Me know him, local man. Him have a band dat play in di different taverns an on di streets. Him sufferin wid a broken heart. Him woman die an lef him wid twelve children an a young sister-in-law. Me didn't want to tell him no, so me move aside an let him in. Glory sleep pon di pallet. Me move her to di far side an lay down an lift up me skirt. Me was tired. As him on top of me, we move quiet, but every now an den she would wake up an moan. Him would have to stop, me would have to get up an rock she back to sleep. Den we would start again; den she would wake again, bawlin. It was like she know. Finally, di only way we could finish was for me to put she down nex to we an hold on to her hand, to keep her asleep. She was cold because she kick off di covers. I never figet dat feelin. Her cold little han, an Rigo pushin in and out of me. Me never like it. Rigo never say nuttin. Him jus wait patiently – lucky it was him an not one a dem odda kind of man. But me, when him leave, me have to be sick; me know it was di house callin me home. After dat, me have to leave. So we pack up an go back.

Me tink dat is why Glory turn out di way she did. She see too much.

Not many women make it off di Alley. Some die, some move away, some leff on boats wid di sailors, followin promise dat me sure never happen. But none become respectable. None become part of di town; di good ladies would not have it. Every now an den some white woman, bored wid her sof' life, would come an try to educate us. One want fi set up school for di children. Hate white woman. Even more dangerous dan white man. Is dem dat hate us like poison, is dem dat figet we sell fi keep dem husband dick in practice, or keep away di children dem don't want. Dat is di real reason dem try fi help us. Dem really want we out. Dey was one called Madam Hento. Me nuh know what her problem, but she hate us. She had dat look on she face like she smell sumting stink. After a while di lampi fish smell didn't affect us. Well Madam Hento turn up in a carriage, wid a lace handkerchief at she nose. When she step out di carriage, she faint. Her driver had to hole her up at di same time as trying fi not touch her. A black man wid him hands on a white woman – him coulda hang fi dat. Den a next carriage turn up an a man run out an grab hold of di wailin woman an push away di driver. Well him let go an di woman fall back pon di ground. We stand round an laugh. Den we stop because we know di poor man goin die dat day. Madam Hento never come back. Never know what happen to di driver but some weeks later a body was found floatin in di harbour, but dat not unusual. Dey was bodies all di time. It was always di talk.

..."Not anodda one. Why dem choose here fi lan pan?"

"Me no know, but dem say it was as big as a house."

"Dat is chupidness, big as a house, cyant go so."
"Is di water blow dem up so so so."
"Is true, me see for me self."
"Yuh?"
"Yes."
"But you is as bline as a bat."
"Ah who seh so?"
"A me, an if yuh can fine me, me go bus yuh arse."
"But where it come from?"
"Where any a dem come from, dem jus come."
"Yes, but why here? Long as me member, always dem come ya. Me modder say dat her modder fine one."
"No!"
"Yes, dat is why me fam'ly have such bad luck."
"A true, all a you family ugly like monkey."
"A true."
"Shut you mout."
"But she never go to di bush an bury some milk an blood under di tree?"
"Dat not workin for everybody."
"Yes man, it work."
"How you know?"
"Well…"
"But what about dis one? Man or woman?"
"Man."
"Maybe a island man coming back to him home."
"Could be. If dat was to happen, not a ship could pass, how di harbour full!"
"But it always bout dis time."
"True."
"Me feel say it mus be sailor fall overboard an nobody know."
"Nobody care."
"Funny. Why dem always end up here?"
"Becas di place so full a badness dat's why."
"Shut yuh mout."
"A true."
"Is like di place invite all di bad people from everywhere an den it kill dem off."

"Poor souls, floatin around, lookin for somewhere to dock."
"Me tell yuh di island curse."
"Wa?"
"Oh stop yuh noise!"
"A di troot me a talk. Dis place curse."
"Alright den prove it."
"Is what yuh a say? How many bodies is dat since Christmas?"
"Two."
"T'ree."
"No, a four."
"A lie yuh a tell."
"Is true."
"Kiss me hemfront, so many?"
"Eehee."
"Yuh no have to look far to see seh dat Church curse."
"Is how yuh mean?"
"Look at we life, to backfoot."
"Dat mean all a we curse?"
"True."
"If we curse, so everybody else."
"True."
"I goin tek sumtin an choke out yuh life; all me fam'ly look good."

It could have been him, for we never see him again. Sometime dey was sailors, sometime dey was woman – nobody know where dem from. Seem like Church just attract dem. Death lived alongside us den. And see me yah!

SECOND MOVEMENT

The town square, Marshall's office.

Marshall, looking out of his window

Goddamn these people, these godforsaken people, what the woman who looked after me would call "dutty, lazy neagah" people. What do they want now? Always demonstrating, always protesting. Life's unfair. The laughter of Ham ringing in their ears. Want everything handed to them on a silver platter. Get them to do anything you have to beat them with a stick. What they're used to. Feel tired just seeing them outside the court house. Maybe it's time to retire. My back's not straight, my arms and hands give me trouble. But can't sit down all day long waiting to die. This place would go to hell. I'll die doing this. They'll find me with a knife sticking out my back.

Should be happy she's gone. One less thing to worry bout, but somehow, I'll miss her. Only in the way you miss an old dog you'll miss patting. I'll look in later. Would look bad for me to go to the funeral of such a woman. My breath feels easier, without that thorn. Feel lighter. What to do?

But if is not one thing is another. My informants tell me of this man inciting rebellion and violence. He's not from here. Don't know where him from. One of them educated browns from the mainland, come to tell us how to live and who to be. We know where we are, we know who we are. Don't need some young pup trying to change things. Well he's going to meet trouble today. Thought I saw that mad girl, Loo. What's she doing here? The funeral can't be over, so how come she's here? But that girl don't know where she is. Well, if she's not careful she's going to get the same treatment as the rest of them.

Seduce always hated me. She looked on me with contempt,

ever since the first time I saw her. She walk through the town like she own it. But she didn't. I did. And on that day I prove it.

It's not just here. All across these islands people demonstratin. Talk of revolution an kicking the white people out. Not many of them left since di big bangarang. No doubt they thought the funeral would be a distraction, that we'd be watching that instead of him and his mob of pimps, dockworkers, beggars and back-to-Africans. Thought they could spit out their lies and confusion without interruption. This island's stood quiet for many years and that's down to me. This young upstart, this agitator, what does he hope to gain? Freedom for Blacks? They wouldn't know what to do with it.

I know the Lampis have gone to Seduce's house, come out from their hiding places, even though Glory asked me to forbid them. There'll be another call out there, for sure. Blacks and plenty rum ent a good combination. Somebody gets hurt. Somebody always gets hurt. She'd like that. Pain – in her name.

Never fit in here. When I was younger I wanted her to love me. Don't know if I loved her, but I wanted her to love me. Instead she needed me. Not the same thing. She was beneath me – too Black. I always tell her so, but I wanted her to feel pain for me. Like the ole washerwoman that kept for me did feel the pain for my farder. But Seduce never did. If it was me being buried today, she'd be on the cane rum. I'll find release another way.

Ha, there's the lieutenant gatherin his men outside, at the top of the courthouse steps. I had to call them in. My informants say this man's been here for weeks. Who does he think he is? I've worked too hard for what I have. My office, my station. I'm not the raggle-taggle, red, dirty houseboy that sleep with the dogs they all used to feel sorry for, feed with table-scraps.

"Officers! Attention!" Someone will get hurt today. Someone always gets hurt. What is wrong wid them? Always wanting to protest. Every minute, complainin, nothin good enough for them. Should have kept them in chains.

"Make ready! Blue watch to the roof, Troffeau and Gardi, take the steps! Let's show these people who's in charge. Advance!"

Loo

"We fed up a dis!"

"What dem tek we for?"

"We starve; dem laugh."

When we run from di funeral dis morning, we fine ourselves in di middle of town. Don't know why. We see a crowd an start tinkin we back at Nanny funeral. When we blink an let di salt wata fall from we eye, we see dat it's a different crowd. A gathering, black, white and brown, in front a di court house. Big, white, chupid place – too much for dis small square. No need for sumtin so big. We only a small island. One of di few white people buildings we left standing after di bangarang. We see dat two people is standing on di top steps. People we don't recognise, an das a surprise becas we know everybody. She behine him, up the steps, a big hat coverin her pale face from the sun, her eyes down. His smooth skin invite us.

Him shouting, di crowd cheerin. We creep closer to hear what him sayin, for we was always nosy.

"Mek dem come!"

"Me no see no rich man here."

"That is right, my brothers, it is only we that suffer. We may have dashed most of them out in di big bangarang, but from across the sea they still pullin the strings. What I'm talking about is independence." Everybody start cheer an clap.

"Who needs the white man, doin nothing but reaping the benefits of our sweat? What we need is land where the food we grow on it belongs to us."

More cheerin, more clappin.

"Slavery is still here my brothers. One hundred years has changed nothing. What has the white man's freedom given us?

Well, I'll tell you now – hold on now – here is the news: nuttin! White man's freedom equals black man's slavery."

The noise in our ears frightens us. We do not like to be frighten. Like when we went to Nanny's room. Don't know why, jus feel so. When we first see her face, ashy, drawn tight, her mout open, we tink she dead.

… "Come in child – all ah you – come in. What's wrong?"

"Nuttin, we fine."

"Me soon gone. You know dat?"

"Yes, we know." Dat was Nanny, always telling us sumting we already know. We wander around di room, touching tings, bottles, bowls wid herbs in, liquids dat smell of sky an life, small mirrors dat only show part of we face.

"As nutty as a fruit cake, dat's what you is. Gone clear. Me wish me neva tell you bout Lucretia. It mek you mad."

"What?"

"You names, you names… Maybe no one should be call so, it put di curse pan yuh."

"Is not a curse."

"Is not a blessin."

"Is life, Nanny."

"But is not yours, mad gyal!"

"We not mad. Why d'you say such tings, evil ole woman?"

"Hah! What you know bout evil? You is a chile in a big woman body, walkin roun chatting to youself. What goin happen to you? Nanny soon gone." We sit on her bed til she close she eyes.

"Me tyard, chile. Want to go."

"Den go."

"But we still have much to do."

"To do?"

She clap her maaga lips togedda, her tongue pushin out like a lizard.

"You is a chile in a woman's body. A woman dat is getting on too. You getting ole!"

"And you goin to die."

She laugh and cough, choke on she own bile.

"You mus be ready."

"We are ready."

"No, yuh mus be free. When yuh ready, go fine me farder. Him inna di bush, go fine him. He will help yuh."

"He is of no more use dan us!"

"Dat's it my girl, spit you fire, hehe, dere is nobody better dan us."

"Nobody!"

She slowly turn her wata eye to di window, fi look at di town and when she speak, her voice lose its bass, it was high and shart.

"But, growin ole, layin here, me get to fine out, he is part of us."

"We don' need help, Nanny, we..."

"Do as I say!" Her voice raspin in the middle of her body, everyting in her is holdin onto she breath. Dat is why she in pain. We know dis.

"Is di pain bad, Nanny?"

"Go away chile, me cyant hardly talk!"

We go. But when me hear di sound of she pain, we come back. The fight is ugly, we do not wish to see the fight.

We can see where dis rally goin. Him still talking, jumpin from one foot to di odda, like we in church, lovin di soun of him voice.

"Time to cut loose. They step out of their country, they tief and pillage, rape the land an destroy the people. And infect us with their diseases. When slavery done, they got paid compensation for our bodies; we got nothing for the work they stole from us. When they finally leave, we left with nothing. Now their lackies sell us out for their own comfortable ends, to furnish their backsides and line their pockets. When they don't want us no more, then they dash us aside like we was Lampi."

"Dat's right."

"Amen."

Why dis man we don't know feel to look at we when him say Lampi?

"It's like they stealin you woman, use her up an then give her back to you, wasted, wash out. You don't want them after that. What use is she to you after that?"

"A true, we don' want dem."

Sometime we feel everybody know about us, an we is naked. Everybody follow him eye an look pan we.

"I say to the government, the foreign rulers, an the police, the agents of our oppressors, cut we loose, cut we loose!"

"Cut we loose, cut we loose!" the crowd shout. We start shoutin too, for we always like to shout. Nanny seh is so her modder used to do, jus shout. We di only woman dere. We don't mind; man hold no fear for us, dey always more scared of us than we of dem. Dem turning round an looking at we again.

"What you doin here, gyal?"

We never know what to say, so we say, "Cut we to rass loose!"

Dem all laugh at di back. Man up front stop talking fi a heartbeat, lookin on we again. Den, him carry on. His voice like honey, drippin an bubblin over hot rock. We wonder what it would be like to have his voice drip an bubble over we.

"To be a Black man is to be a proud man. We must stand up for ourselves. Slavery done, brothers, slavery done. They cannot justify our oppression any longer. How many more years must we stand by and watch ship after ship take away our natural resources. Take away the food from our children's mouths while we struggle?"

"No!"

"No, no!"

"Yuh talk di troot, my brodda."

"Time run out."

"Cut we loose!"

"Dat's right."

"Dis bwoy can talk."

"Anybody know him people?"

"No."

"No, me nuh know."

"You don't look like *you* struggling too bad." We don't know why we say dat. Is like we lips have a mine of dem own.

Everybody turning again to stare pan we.

"I, er, couldn't hear you, sister. You have something to contribute? If so I will gladly..."

"You hear what we say fine. And you an we is no relation."

A few laugh. We see dat some a dem drunk. Di crowd getting bigger, an instead of bein jus outside it, we fine ourselves in di middle. Honey Rock looks like he want to box us. He turn to look at the woman wid he, like she can help him, but you can tell from she face, she stop helpin him long time.

"Where you from?" Di crowd look like dem just tink di same question.

"What does that have to do with anything, sister?"

"We never see you before, we know everyone here."

"From the mainland."

Is like everybody surprise.

"Born dere, bred dere?"

"Yes."

Den somebody shout up, "What you know bout we struggle?"

"Dem uppity mainland blacks lef we far behind, man."

"Yes."

"What him doin here anyway?"

"No listen to him!"

"Shut up nuh. Jus cos you sister send you a money when she member you alive, you tink we must lick up to dem?"

Honey Rock fight back.

"You see, brothers, this is what di white man want. This is the ultimate goal of the white man. They want us to fight each odda, so that we forget that they refuse to pay us a decent price for our goods. Do not fall into their trap."

Crowd mumbling, an den it is turnin to shouts, an we know why before we see dem. We hear a whistle an suddenly we surround by di police. Dem comin out of dem hiding places, up from di empty market, up di road towards di court house. Dem on di roof an at di windows, pourin out of di court house an standin silently on di top steps.

"Him set we up."

"Di foreigner know bout dis."

"Don't chat foolishness, we know whose work dis is."

"Did dat mad gyal bring dem?"

Crowd pushin each odda, a creepin feelin of fear runnin troo dem. It pass from one to di odda like electricity. It has dem root to di spot.

It makes us sad for di people; the day has miss di point. Then we remember Nanny gone. It mek di back of we neck turn cold. Nanny gone. We start pushin people out di way. We have no wish to be touched. We arready feelin too much. Crowd start movin close in togedder, squashin me in di middle. Some try to grab after us. We never like to be trapped so we start pushin man over. Need to keep movin, keep workin our way out. We reach di police line. Someone grab hold of we hair and dey tryin to pull we to di groun. Di grip is loose an we see Honey Rock has slap up a di man dat hold onto we. He helps us stand. His woman has melted away.

"Brothers dis is what dem want. Stand your ground. Be men, not cowards. Be men. Stand your ground!"

Him is shouting into fear. Him no know what is swooping down pon we, from di top of di court house steps. Di crowd have abandon him, dey rushin forward, trying to flee. If we didn't move, we would be crush. Him hold we han. We run wid what feel like di whole islan behine us, we run though di market til we get to watch from di edge of di road. We see di police slowly come down di stairs and at di same time from up di road. Di crowd is blocked in. Di screamin is almost more dan we can bear. We try to squeeze his han but it has let go of us and is gone. Honey Rock has gone. We wonder how him move so fast.

Gettin outside di crowd an turnin back we see Marshall swoopin down like di big John Crow him is, doin what him love bes', crackin heads. Dis why him not at Nanny funeral. He must be missin her, an every man dere goin feel it. Every kick in di seed, every punch in di belly, every break in a han or foot, every shoulder dat dislocate will send him message to her. We turn an run. We have no wish for violence today. We want to see Nanny. We go to di old Lampi shed on di edge of di dock but she ent there. The sheds are empty an hollow. We can hear the laughter, the tears and di moaning agony of women forgotten an left to rot. The smell, small and losin power, but still there, remind us of Nanny. So we leave di sheds and walk up behind dem, to go lookin for weselves in di bush, where Nanny said we would be waitin. Sweat builds in the dips of our back. We feel weselves an no other. Maybe he could not come. We know the callin. It feel like an old blanket dat smell of we people, dat we use to cover us. We know the callin and ever since childhood we bear witness. Sitting on the boundary rock we close our eyes an close out the light and hear the noise dat still fill every space in us, aroun us…

And in di flow of the time of the great ships, of feeding sharks wid our flesh, of rough white fingers pushed into us, white babies at our black breast, of ropes around our necks, of pain and anger dat is as big an wide as di sea we travelled on, tiny grains of stone stick under we fingernails.

THIRD MOVEMENT

Outside Seduce's house

The Lampis

"Biggest funeral Church Island ever see."

"Is true."

"Me never tink me would see di day when Miss Seduce dead."

"A true, she was an ole woman when me was a gyal, an now me ole, cyant even chew food, an til recent she still strong."

"Well, some say her farder was a bush man."

"Yes, so dem say."

"Dem long livers."

"She just decide to leave."

"A true."

"Yes, when you ready, you ready, an she mussa been ready."

"Dat ole gyal was di best Lampi dis place ever know."

"Is true."

"Dey wasn't nuttin she wouldn' do fi di rest of we."

"How so?"

"Well, me hear seh one time, dey was a man and he tek set pon di Lampis. Back in the days when we use to cook di stinkin fish on di shore. All di Lampis complainin bout him an even though Sed was in di duppy house, she still come by from time to time. Well, all of us complainin bout dis man. Him wicked, wicked, wicked."

"Filthy, dirty man."

"Eee heee, him was a beater, a killer of women, an untame devil, dat should a garn long time."

"Yes, him love to lick woman pan a full moon."

"Don't matter to him a who."

"If it wasn't us, was him wife."

"Dat's right."

"Beat dem, rape dem. Diamond swear dat him try to piss pan she."

"Lard!"

"Well all di Lampis complain. We even go an talk to Marshall."

"What?"

"Him just as bad."

"True."

"Well, we go to Miss Seduce fi help. She say leave it to her. Dat was dat. Nobody see di dirty man again."

"You tink she kill him?"

"No mus. Cut off him johnson an bury him!"

"Maybe, maybe, she just send him out to di bush, mek her people deal wid him."

"Is Sed put a stop to it."

"True."

"Dat's right."

"How she always do, how it's always been done, since before time..."

"Once a man start give lick, it come in like him a darg. Once a man taste blood, him crave it, long fi it, find ways and ways fi get it."

"True."

"Me hear dat she did go and cuss out Marshall as well."

"True."

"Why?"

"Cos him shoulda protec us, not usin us fi satisfy himself and then don't do nuttin to help."

"What you expec? Is a man. Dem always take care of dey own."

"A true."

"An we take care of we own."

"Dat Marshall ent human."

"Is how come him still livin?"

"Dem say him protec."

"Dat wouldn't surprise me. Dat man would sell him nanny."

"Di spirits dem too free in dis house."
"Di dead house?"
"You see dem?"
"Everywhere yuh turn roun yah."
"Is how Miss Seduce put up wid dem?"
"Dem had she pickney fi company."
"Poor souls."
"Watch di sky, sisters, look up an watch di sky. Sun still high, moon waiting."
"Oh shut up you mout, you have to listen within."
"No, we mus listen widout."
"Eh?"
"Hear dem, cyant you hear dem?"
"No, dem mout fulla Sed food."
"Dem eat she bread an no know how it mek."
"Di day move and so mus we."
"Me can hear dem, but dem nuh seh nuttin."
"Yes, dem a seh sumptin, you jus haffi listen."
"Peel-head jankrow sit up inna tree top."
"Waitin, watchin, waitin."
"Beat di drum."
"Let it rock yuh soul."
"Beat out di drum."
"Hear you spirit sing."
"To di soun a yuh heart."
"Beat di drum."
"To move yuh foot."
"Beat out di time."
"Di time comin."
"Beat out yuh secret."
"Secrets comin."

Seduce

Where Loo? Me sight stretch far, but still cyant feel her.

Di house don't tek to me blood. It push me out like a jacket chile. Expel me. Me haffi be a woman to return. And return me did, belly out to here, Glory in tow. At first me still work in town, mek di trek every day, drop off Glory to di small church in between di house an di town dat turn into di school in di week, an had every child in the area.

Dis was di plantation house, every district have one. It was always here, lookin down at di town below and den out to di sea beyond. Di slaves burn most of it down, but lef this part. Dis house see too much death. Some seh dat is what wrong wid it. It was a place where people come to die. An look, dem still bout di place.

Dey leave dem mark, dem white people, holy god, dem leave dey mark! All across di islands, skeleton houses, not ready to die, resting on we bones. Every time you look, look like di house move, tryin to avoid me gaze an keep its secrets. But it did always share its secrets wid Glory, always.

No one from around know fi true how me grandmodder get di house doh rumour fly from one mout to di odda. A doctor live here once. Wedda him real or a horse doctor, who knows? Dem seh him treat all di white ladies wid sof words an gentle squeezes. Dey come to him rooms an di doors shut pon dem husbands. He treat all di Black people as if dey had di clap, young an old. Mus be nuff people dat di quack kill off. Some seh me grandmodder steal to get di house. Now, dere is a lot of stories bout me grandmodder. Some say she was a juju woman, but she too Christian fi dat, Church of Latter Day Holy Nazarene. Blood, fire and death, vengeance and retribution. A clear woman, wid blue eyes, set adrift in a sea of blackness, to her dismay an disgust. Dat was she. She seh she was a woman from di land, one of di originals, dat is what she tell me.

Den me hear seh dat before di doctor, di house belong to Mama Pearl's half cousin, fam'ly, a man from round yah, jus out a slavery. Dem hang him, from di hanging tree dat always 'tan at di mout of any town. He beat a white man for daring to approach him wife. Jus freed, him feel him have di right, an di whites try to run di free blacks outta town after dat. Dey didn't like dem parading dem freeness. Him hang from di same tree as Lucretia, some seh. Man don't do so well in dis ya fam'ly. How di docta get di house from she cousin, me nuh know, but mussa be why Mama Pearl feel she have di right.

Story, story, from lie to troot and back again.

So how it come to Mama Pearl? Years after she die and me had been in town long time, me work it out. Me was tending me cookin fire an it come to me. She kill di docta fi di house. Such is we legacy. Murda run troo we like salt. An when me tink bout it, di breath heave inna me ches, an me tink she spirit close roun me, an jus fi a moment, it tek way di fear an di hatred me carry fi she – or any one a dem useless feelins. Me tink she did see off di wotless ole doctor, an tek him house an me grateful. How could me jus lef it so when she had done so much to get it?

Di house contain me hist'ry, everyting bout it: di rooms, where di light come in troo di windows and an choose to sit; di curve of di walls, di shadows in di corners; di massive kitchen – not many kitchen indoors in dem days. An di hill it stand pon. Di hill wid di curve of a woman and di secrets of a man. That tell me more dan anyting what kinda house it was. Di shape an colour a di soil. Dis where me born. Dis where me die. Sumtin right bout dat. Sumtin right. Bartroom outside, a well fi draw water, an a likkle shed fi wash yuhself. Out back was di toilet, a deep hole in di ground, dat had to be cleaned by a boy. Glory put a bartroom in di house. Shittin near you food not right.

Dem say dat to get rid a duppy you have to tell dem dutty bad word. Well, me was Lampi, so dere was no dutty bad word you can teach me dat me don't arready know. When we move back to di house me light frankincense an put down a piece a bad word in every room. Glory laugh. Me an Glory move from room to room, me cursin, she laughin. Den me had to think. Me never see dem, but lookin at Glory me know dem wid her, dat dey protect her. Big Mama Pearl Before Swine say dat her people under di ground here. Di first ones bury deep under di foundation. An den Likkle Pearl, me modder, bury up so at di back a di house, an Big Mama Pearl not far from she. You mus live near you people. Widdout dem protec yuh, yuh loss. Never feel dat when me younger; me know better now.

Me hear seh, over yonda way, in di next distric, the O'Dells go turn dem house into hotel. You hear dat, Mamma Pearl? Hotel. So, yuh finish yuh hardship an labour fi turn roun an serve dem tea an hot chocolate, only dis time dem a pay you pittance for servin dem. What a way di worl turn. Serving eggs over we eyes, tea an coffee over we hearts.

Di house claim Glory for its own. You could tell all now, so many years later, she still feel it, still ah mess wid di duppy dem, cept she call it sumting and every one call it sumting an dat mek it right. Still, di livin ent worth botherin wid. She have dat way bout her from long time. Lissen to her nuh.

Glory

What a way people pretendin to be sad. Where is Loo? Why can't dat gyal stay in one place?

Even in di bright sunshine dis place dark. Me always see di darkness lurkin in di middle. No one else could, an if dem did, dem pretend not to, like now. Pretendin to be mournin her when dem hatred for she run so deep dey don't even know how it start, or where it came from, or how it go end. Mama could see but she chose not to see.

On di mainland di light so bright, di brightness take over and dry you out. Everyone brittle and hard. When me a child, di life me lead not good fi a child. Me just end up spoilin my own, trying fi win dem back from Mumma afta she fine a way to keep dem spirit from me. An now Loo has run off, and Son – me don't know where him is. An he never have a woman. Not for long. Me no know why.

Seduce always touch me too much, but widout wanting me near her. Di touchin was for her, not for me and, oh Lord, she talk to me too much. I was always her fren, not her child. Always she want me to look after her. I don't think it start that way in she mind, but that is how it end up and she never did anything to stop it. It suit her. I got to dat point when I couldn't do it any more, me was close to death or madness. That is why me run to di mainland. She did hate me for dat.

When di duppy dem left me, so little was left, me start disappear. Each day me get smaller an smaller. Not like losin weight but actually missin body parts. Me lose me left hand for months and when me feel di right one was goin, me jump on a ship wid di first sailor that show any interest in me. I was not Seduce daughta, I was meself. Seduce always hate sailors because of her life before. She despise dem and from when Jono show up at di door she want to run him, but I grab him with both hand, dig my nails in along wid my life – an didn't stop to take a good look at di man.

Me know me hurt her but she never should've had me – even dat was jus proof of she power. She choose di seed, she always tell me dat – dat dere are ways you can rid youself of di seed you don't want. She was not di motherin kind. She only had me to extend sheself, an look, she live so long she didn't need extendin. I always live under her shadow; it was always too strong for me. Everybody loved her, hated her, had her. Now she dead, me tink she was fightin she own shadows, like Grandma Likkle Pearl. Seduce spend her life touchin people on a purpose, not on a purpose. Me? I spend me time avoiding dem. Dat is why me marry di first man me let touch me – an look how him was a sailor, because him spirit shipwreck. Him like me modder – bad for people around him, bad for people dat care bout him, like sweet tastin poison. Him nuh know how fi love, jus take. I struggle so hard to be free of her I ran into di arms of a man jus like her. An, coo-coo, dey couldn't stand each other. Too same same. Dey must have seen demselves in each odda and all dem want is me time and love. But fi true, me don't have enough to give.

Before we move back to dis house, when we live at Paradise Alley, me die a thousand times. Dis when me know that I could lose myself. Men come to di door sometimes. If we bruk she send me out to play wid di odda kids or send de man to Lucy up di road. Most time she try to keep it away from me, but when man drunk, lookin for her, lookin you up an down like to say a six-year-ole chile would do, it mek you skin crawl. An crawl it did. She seh she want a better life for us. Me don't tink she tinkin about us at all. How could she have expose me to dat? Sometimes di noises from di shack and di shacks all around mek me vomit. Once a sailor came to di door, swayin, stink, white. "Is your beautiful mother at home?"

"No, she dead." I don't know why me say dat. Me nearly dead when she fine out. I got di biggest backsiding ever.

Di mainland was a mistake. Trap myself wid a man dat need even more dan me children.

"Where's my food, Glory? Can't find my shirt, you clean dem boots yet? Not like you mother, are you?"

Di sins of di mother must come to di daughter, dat is what him use to say. Him see me modder in me after all. And dat is how he treat me, like a ole whore, use to his ways. But I never got use to it, never. I was clean, like a clean towel dat him use to wipe himself wid. Now, so many years after him dead, I can see how confuse him was. All Black people on di mainlan lost. Dem live dere, dem grow dere, all dem really know bout is cleaning up white people mess. All when me was dere, every other black person me know clean up mess. Seduce was right bout dat. How many children learn about pride inna place like dat? All dem learn to do is keep dem head down. If it wasn't surrounding yuh, it was at home. Jono couldn't remember his people or where him from. He choose to forget dem. He was still a sailor when we marry; he leave me for months on me own. Den turn up an expec everyting to be di same. God knows how many woman he had. Di only reason me manage to stay alive is because he wasn't dere. Him leave di navy because him hurt him foot. Dat was my fault as well. Him get a job on the new railways, jus doin di same ting he did as a sailor. Clear up after dem, look after dem, mek sure dat dey did not see themselves clearly.

When me first see him, Lord, Jono look like di night smilin. Mama kept me so close she didn't notice I was getting old. She didn't understand why I could love a man so black. But she never love any man. He loved di way me look, make him feel like he sleepin wid a white woman. When I tink bout it now, maybe wid every time, him getting him own back.

... "Never know a girl like yuh."

"What's that?"

"You're so quiet. I like dat."

We lookin at di sea. The sun sinkin away. Di day I met him I had run from di house – another fight wid me mumma. I ran to di market an dere him was, him an he sailor friend, by Inchos rum shop. Him look different, quiet, like him tinkin hard, hard, hard. I like dat. Not like di island man. Everyting dem know, yuh know, every ting dem tink, yuh tink – an well before dem. I like it dat him look like him was tinkin an me never know what about. If only me did know it was di poison darkness in his mind dat was hidin itself.

Me used to meet him at di clearing behind di house. Me heart would beat – don't know if it was for him or me. I tink now it was for me. I know me mumma know, but we play a merry dance wid each odda. She'd watch me run out of di house to meet him, shake her head an suck she teet. But me was nearing me thirties by dis point. He was twenty-two.

"You waitin long?"

"Forever not too long to wait for you."

Me know dis was rubbish, but when me ever get dat kind of attention? Dat was reserved for me mumma.

"Where do you want to go?"

"Anywhere."

"Well, why don't we stay here?"

"Here? Me mumma could catch us."

"You a little old to be worrying about your mumma."

"It's not jus dat, I don't like it here."

"Why?"

"No, Jono." I walk off. "Don't like dat clearing, always mek me shiver."

"Okay, let's walk."

He held me han. I never like dat but me let him.

"What's the matter, Glory?"

"Oh, nuttin. Me just… there's tings dat should not be talk about. Yuh tink me chupid an backward?"

"No, just a little too mysterious."

"Me?"

Me laugh. All me life people look at me and not see me.

"Tell me why you so quiet. I hope you thinking about me."

"No." We laugh but him eyes not smiling.

"What is the name of this flower?"

"Little Passion." I become embarrass.

He grab me han. "Every time you look at it, smell it, touch it, you must think of me."

"OK."

"No, look at me, look at it." He wouldn't let go. "Think about how it looks, the purple, the red, the yellow centre."

He pull me han roun him and hold on to me neck back. "Can you see why it's called Little Passion. Can you see?"

"Yes."

"Oh I'm sorry." He let go den and had di look of a child scared of getting cuss. "What am I doing? You see that's what you do to me. My name should be Little Passion. It's just that I've never been wid anyone like you." He touched me all over, gentle, as if I would break. "God must've sent you to me."

We clung to each other. I couldn't believe the way he loved me. It was like him didn't see me modder at all.

...What di hell all dese people here for? What dem sayin goodbye to? Look at di men dem. The sight bring on dem old feelings of wanting to be sick. So what? Dey sayin goodbye to di old Lampi Queen. Dat ole hole. I don't tink she ever like any of dem, let alone love dem. What di women hopin to see? Just mekkin sure she dead. Mekkin sure dem is still alive. So many years of walkin into a room an everybody stop an look at me, like dirt beneath dem shoes. Look, dere goes di daughter of di Lampi Queen – surprise she not Lampi too. And hear di old Lampis left from me modder's days getting drunk outside. What dem have to laugh about?

Seduce

Mek me tell how it was in dem Lampi days.

When me was thirteen, me lef di house. After me grandmodder pass, what was dere to stay for? She always tell me dat me come from mud an dirt. I decide to go back dere. She use to sing dat my birth was di reason why she pickney dead. She look at me an mek me wash so many times a day, it mek me raw. Couldn't stan di house so when she pass, me come into town. When me first workin as a Lampi me tink it was to cook fish. But to say you is Lampi is to say you is a whore, but it was one of di few jobs dat come wid a roof over you head.

... "Eh gyal, yuh look good, eeh."

"Me coulda drink out you bart."

"Whooo, you modder know you out?"

"How much?"

"What dem sayin?"

"Pay dem no mine, you get used to it."

"What you doin roun here?"

"Lookin fi work."

"Yuh? But you too small. How old yuh is?"

"Eighteen."

"Yuh lie."

"A lie yuh a tell."

Before me know what goin on, me fist come out an tump down one of dem. Sometime me tink me body have him own mind. All di odda girls fall down laughin and then a really big, dark one – me figet her name – take me aside.

"What you doin here, chile. Dangerous round here."

"A woman at di market tell me is here me can look fi work."

"You know what we do, chile?"
"Me know. Cook lampi."
"You can tek di smell?"
"Can yuh tek di smell of you modder?"
She laugh. She was so tall, she stoopin down to hear me and her skin was di darkest blue-black of di sky before daybreak. Her face show goodness. I wonder now why she dere. Well, we all have a story to tell, nuh true? Back den, me not interested in anybody else's.
"All right, chile, alright. If you want a job you got one, but is backbreakin labour."
"True."
Dey all laugh. Dey seem good natured. Not a ting like what me hear. Di two big vats stand in a kind of cradle, wid ladders rigged up so dat we could climb up to cook di fish an add di seasoning an spice. Di spice sacks so big an heavy, tek two of we to climb up dem ladders an pour it in. Dere was two large tree trunk on each side so di vat could be rock and pour out an laid out onto di cooling trays. Di Lampis was famous amongst all di islands. Dey was me firs real fam'ly. Me grandmodder try, but she too full a anger fi di worl. Dem was loud, rambunctious, filthy women, wid not much to lose, cookin di stinkin fish, ready to be taken all over di world. Dem use to say dat even di king of England eat lampi. Not anymore, dat deh tradition dead.
In dem days nobody really want to be anyting. Dem jus do. No one want fi be sailor, black or white. In dem days yuh come sailor because yuh get catch committing some crime, yuh poor or in di wrong place at di wrong time and dat was dat. Be a sailor or hang. Dem sailors rough. Far from home, months, years at sea, desperate. Like me say, if some had done nuttin, some was jus plain criminal. Dey was big, rough, frowsy lookin, stink from months at sea, an hungry fi anyting. Ships dem days was places to die in if you poor. Dem use to be mek from wood. Great long ships wid thousands of ropes and sails dat block out di sun.
What me didn't know is dat all di Lampi dem – must have been t'irty of them – was seeing di sailors at night. Dat was

consider a part of di job. Cookin di lampi only give yuh so much money, fuckin di sailors is what put food on yuh table. But me never know dat, or me tink me never know. Back in dem days, a ship use to come every month. Dem come fi coffee, sugar an lampi. We cook an cook, an di lampi was store in a big shed in dem wooden barrels waiting for di ships to come. Behind dem sheds was we quarter. Just wooden shacks, mek out of shipwreck wood. Dem call it Paradise Alley. Dey was all colour a pickney everywhere. If yuh lucky yuh get to send dem away to relatives in di country. What a life! Back in dem days everyone was like a piece of trash – trow it away when yuh done wid it. Especially women an children.

Dem tek me to see di foreman. Dem days di white people was still here. Dem still rule all now, but not inna me eyeline, jus in we spirit. Di foreman name Kenzo, don't know what country him from, but him white skin have a yellow tinge. Too much rum, too much sex. Him in charge of di Lampis, must have been in him fifties den. When me fine out me cry an cry an cry. Dem didn't give me no option, an me too fraid to back out. Pride will kill you. It nearly kill me. Me move into di only empty shack next to di dark woman. Wish me could remember she name. She kinda look after me. Di firs time me bleed, she tek me to sit in di sea, an di sea salt wata run wid me eye salt wata, an me did feel what me granmumma tell me all along.

Me meet man from all over. Come from places me never hear bout, some places me still know nuttin about. In between cookin di fish, you tek sailors back to you shack. An if dey was no sailors, dey was always a few white men an always di locals. Black man get to us last. Some a dem couldn't quite believe it. Dem nuh know what fi do. Coffee an sugar farmers always rich; dey never come to di sheds. Dem no change from slavery done, so dey still tek dem pick of dem worker. It was di foremans an clerks an such dat come down to di sheds. Don't understand dem white man. Like dem screwin di ting dem hate di most. An funny. Lord, dem could arks yuh fi some strange ting. One man, him di school teacher, use to put on a big nappy an suck on you titty like him was you child. Him easy. Some oddas like to be in pain, or like you to be in pain. All manner a ting. You could be any kind you want to be. If you tough, you go onto di ship. Teks a different kinda woman to do dis. She mus be tired a life. By di time me eighteen me was tired.

Di sailors dem use to send a likkle boat fi us. A few Lampis would jump in an row demselves to di ship. Dis one day only me an Esme go. Esme always go. Di men was waitin an we climb up di ropes an dem pull us in. Dere was many men pon di ship but four took Esme one way; only t'ree wanted me. Me too black. Me start to feel fraid an look fi her, but she give me wink an went troo a door.

Ships have many dark corners, places for people to hide an die. You see dat? Death mek you melancholy. Me never worry when me was alive, but now… I wonder how many people dead an nobody know. Are dem lost? Happy to be forgotten? Yuh live as long as yuh are remembered, isn't dat what dem say? Dat is shegs. You live as long as you ent dead.

Me rememba dis man playin wid himself, grabbing at me. Is me secon or t'ird. Cyant remember. Don't like him, smell funny, him mout lose him teet, cyant feel nuttin. Had a fight dat day wid one a di odda Lampis an me no know, me jus feel tired. Me do one afta di odda. Las one keep shoutin dutty bad words. After a while me start feel fraid. Me tink dat yuh not to notice dem, not to feel dem, but dem suppose to feel yuh, even if dey want to pretend yuh dem sweetheart. I've had dat sometimes, but mostly it's man who want yuh because yuh not dem sweetheart, yuh is far away from dem sweetheart. Dem can treat yuh how dem want. Dem want yuh because yuh black an different. Don't quim look di same, no matter di colour of di woman? Doh me hear dat white woman's is di colour of uncook meat. I haven't seen dat many, not close up, only Fanta. Fanta. Dat is all she know how to say, so me tink it was she name. When di third one was finish, me jump up off di barrel. Me hole out me han, waitin for me money. Dem all start laugh. Me pull out di knife from me garter.

"Little nigger girl, what d'you think you're doing?"

"You'll never get off alive."

"Belo, give her the money."

"Give me di money, me leave *you* alive."

"Ha! You think you can hurt me; you think you can hurt all of us?"

Fear is a good ting; yuh should feel it, know it. You fraid for a reason. Me, me lost me reason.

"Come girl, we only have to shout and what d'you think will happen? You'll be caught."

Di two me do firs' not dat bothered. But di las' one want me dead, want me to be fraid. Yuh get some man like dat, just want woman to be fraid of dem, dat is how dem feel a man. He move round me an di oddas make a space round him. Dem want to watch what him goin to do to me – like dey already know. Him beat me. Not di firs time me tek a beatin, but was di las'. He flung me down and sat astride me and use him fists as hammers. Me tink dat me was goin die dat night. Me struggle. Di knife knock out a me han, an one a dem kick it away, so me couldn't reach it. He start to tear at me, but him already spent. Him want to humble me, to hear me cry, to beg him. Me feel fi a moment me better off dead. Him slump on top of me, too tired, too drunk. Me fine di strent to bite him. Me don't know if it was him ear or him cheek. Me feel di flesh tear way from him; salty taste of blood fill me mout. Him scream an me jump up, fling open di door an run an run. In di tight passages, no light, me runnin don't know where me goin, tryin to avoid di dark places. Know me should keep goin up. Buck up on man, him didn't stop me. Mek me tink how many woman dem see, screamin, bleedin, tryin to survive. Me could hear dem followin, shoutin what dem goin do wid me. Me fling open a door. Have to step back. Di smell mek me want to vomit. Me stare into di gloom an di stench, had to put me han ova me nose, but me could jus mek out dat someone was in dere. She move her han to she face an she blink blink blink at di light and start to talk in a language me don't understand. Me figet all di words she teach me, all now I try to think, but dem gone. Dem keep her in a cupboard, use her for whenever dem couldn't reach port. She look young but her eyes was older dan me. Me hear di man comin so me just squeeze in next to her. Me foot step in shit. I had to hole me breath. She start to whisper an try fi push me. Me tink she tryin to save me. Me tell she sshh, sshh. She did an we wait until we hear di runnin and yellin die away. I could feel her eyes lookin at me from di darkness. I crack open di door.

"Come, follow me, follow me." Me use me han to show her what me mean. She look fraid. She start up di whisperin and chantin again.

"Come," me seh, "if me leave you here, you dead." Me tink dat when dem no fine me, dey will pick on her. Maybe dere was odda girls stowed on di ship, but me only know bout dis one. Me hole out me han an she tek it. Lord, she was like a little bird, her head movin quickly, lookin fi danger, an every step she tek di smell of piss an shit an man rise up to me nose. She was di colour a coffee, wid a lot of goat milk, flavour wid molasses. Her hair straight an long, an me tink dat she must've come from di lan where dem eyes is di shape of flowers dat not yet open. Even under di dirt an tears me could see dat she was beautiful.

We jump over di side an swim back to shore. Me had to help her all di way, an twice me nearly let go becas she too heavy. All di time she whisperin, talkin. Don't know how long she on dat ship for. We get to di shore a likkle way up from di bay.

"Look, no one hurtin you now. We stay here till nightfall, yes? Dem sailors go be lookin fi us."

At nightfall I walk off into di jungle. Dere was only one place to go. Me hadn't been back to di house fi years. Den, me neva want to go back dere, but it was di only place me could think of where we could hide. Everybody fraid a di place even den. She follow me, still mekkin noise as she go. When we come to di house she stop. She start to cry, she fall on she knees an look like she prayin. Di sky start rumble, den open up an drop all di water it could fine. Me pull her up but she start to fight me. Me box her an drag her in. Me tink me feel me modder, an wonder if me would see her. But di house don't hole no fear for me, never did. I put some rainwater on di fire in di kitchen. We wash each odda.

It was always like a itch for me, deep inside, dat I could only get rid of through friction. I need di hardness of di wood to destroy dat itch. Till Fanta. Fanta lick at di itch. Me never feel anyting like it. She whisper her tongue in, an soothe dat itch away. She whisper all di time, babblin in her language. I never know what she sayin.

We couldn't go back to Paradise Alley. I know we have to stay until di ship go. We stay in di house for a week or two. One morning me wake up in bed an fine she gone. Don't know if di bush tek her but me would like to tink she gone home.

No one ever see Esme again.

Mikey

I & I do too much fi please woman – me mussa have enough of whatever it is dem need. Me try to block Sed out, but like a beaten darg me always go back. Sed used me. An I and I love her to use me. Sometimes, afterwards, me feel like is I and I need payin. One time me follow her to di beach an tried to force myself onto her, not because me like it dat way – dat is the way of a coward – but because me want to feel whole again. She tek me soul and lef me in pieces.

So, it stay between she and me.

Anodda day we sittin on di beach, just sittin, an I look across at her an me feel betrayed. Her face was so beautiful, so calm an peaceful. Even in moments when me could mek her cry out, mek her laugh, mek her angry, me never mek her look like dat. So me reach ova an stroke she face. I want fi get dat look for meself. She box me han away, come angry again – an funny, me feel more comfortable.

"Yuh happy?"

"When you stop messin inna me face…"

"Come on. Yuh happy?"

"What kine a damn fool question is dat?"

"Well, is not dat hard, you know, Sed. You happy or you not. Dat's all."

"Move from me, Mikey."

"Oh, is real hard fi yuh, ent it?"

"What you want me to say?"

"Nuttin. Di troot."

"Yes."

"Wah?"

"Me seh yes, me happy."

"Liar."

"Well what you want me to say?"

"Just..."

"Alright, alright, no."

"Why?"

"Because you ask me dis damn fool question."

"Don't I give you everyting?"

"Oh shithouse! Me know we was comin to dis."

"Don't me give you everyting?"

"Leave me be."

"What more a woman could want? Don't me tek care of you, you an you silent pickney, give you money, love? Me give you love. Who look afta you when you sick? Who look afta you when you loss di baby?"

"How you dare talk bout dat? Yuh want keep up malice wid me?" She jump up. "Don't yuh eva wash out you mout pan me business."

Dat was it. She run weh. What had I and I done? Arks a simple question. Dat is when me lef foot start swell up.

It took a month fi her to talk to me again. Me couldn't tek it no more. Me go roun her house, me follow her bout, me beg her an beg her. Me neva want to, but pride leave me. Me feel like me have no choice. Seems to me, me beg woman too much, an where it get me? A whole world of trouble. She could be like dat. Hard. Cold. As cole an hard as she is now. Woman not mek to be hard. Is I and I rib. Is me mek she. Woman rule by di moon, man by di sun.

Di coldness start to get to me. Me nuh know how she do it. How could she be dat calm? Woman! I do believe dat woman is here to manipulate man, distract us, mash up and confuse us – as well as demselves. Dem tek an tek an tek. Seduce was a taker. How Glory manage to survive, me nuh know. She tek from her as well. Dat is why she leave. She have no choice. Sed tek from everybody. Di whole ting mek me sick. Me mean really sick. Me chest start tighten up, an likkle men wid big boots go march up an down across me back for days. When me look back pon me life, when me member who I and I was and who I and I come to be, me feel someone tearin out me vein. If it wasn't Seduce, den it was me modder.

Me cyant fault me modder. Tek in washin, grow food fi sell, wash people yard, clean up odda people mess fi sen me to school. She work til she she figet what she ah work for. But all widout love, wid a heart heavy wid loss. And then she wait. She wait fi me to save her. But surely, expectation is a heavy burden fi carry. She wait and wait and what I was to her was di bitteres' disappointment. She want and she want and she want. Dat is why me farder leave. Me modder never like Seduce, hate her like poison, but me tink she never goin like anyone. Nobody good enough. She never stop fi ask herself was she good enough. She use to tell me, "I was on me way to di market wid di orange dat you grandmodder grow. I didn't want to carry dat big ole basket, pack to di top wid orange when me was carrying you, but she say me mus pull me weight. If me want to be part of di fam'ly, me have to do as everybody else. What a woman bitter, you see. Me was never good enough fi her boy, even doh him all a thirty years ole when we marry and I was seventeen. Manfred, Manfred. Hmm! Me hear say she run down some widow woman in her cart dat took a shine to Manny. Dat is what she was like, you grandmodder – mean, hateful an spiteful. Lord!"

Me hear dis story a thousand time; it scorch on me brain wid a slaver's iron. To trap me, to control me, let me know how lucky I was to have her and not my grandmodder. She no know she turn into she modder. I and I sit pan me chair, daring di air round me fi strangle me. Tek way me life, so dat di story stop.

"I was out yasso, me belly so big dat dem did tink it was two or tree me was havin. Tree children at one time run in di fam'ly. Yuh grandmodder had Wilfred, Manfred and Albert. Me prayin fi just di one. But di way how you farder handle me, jus dash me dung and do him business, me neva know dat is how baby mek. Me was seventeen. When di pain start, it draw out all di air from me body and me did feel like me goin dead. Me want scratch out me guts wid me bare han. Me dig me nails into me belly. Me never knew what me doin. Y'know what yuh grandmodder did? Slap me! Straight cross me face til me see stars. Seventeen! Like me know anyting. Tell me if me drop di orange me in trouble. Me tryin so hard not fi let di oranges drop.

Yuh grandmodder start shout at me. Next ting, me fall down. Me start sweat. Di pain! Me never know. Nobody tell me, not a soul, not even me own modder – di treachery! As God me saviour, yuh was rippin me in two. Next ting, blood, blood and water everywhere, flowin down me legs. Me just remember di orange tumble to di ground, rollin in di blood. Yuh grandmodder screamin at me and Manny just standing dere, looking at me like is my fault. The pain, Lord di pain! Dem rush me back home. Yuh take nine days fi come, nine days a blood an sweat an tears. Yuh tear, yuh rip, yuh rip, yuh tear, so dat what was left of me could not bear no more children. Pain til me piss meself. What for? Fi dis! Dere is no greater pain dan you chile turning pan you, lyin to you, betrayin you! Yuh try fi kill me den, an yuh a try fi kill me now. Fi what? All me ever do was love yuh. Feed you, protec yuh."

She voice rose high like a preacher an den crash back down pan me like di waves on di rocks in the bay. Me hear dat for as long as me can remember. Every time she angry wid me, me break sumtin in di house. Neighbours complain bout me flingin rockstone. Me let di food burn on di stove becas me was playin outside. Some girl call round to di house fi see me. Anyting. Dis was her punishment. But it mek me feel like retching up an bring me to me knees. Me would fall to di ground and beg she forgiveness. Me tell she sorry, sorry, sorry over and over again. Den finally, when me couldn't tek no more, me tell her sorry for being born. It tear at me soul to hear di pain me cause her. Me feel guilty bad. When me say sorry she go hug me, an love me up, an tell me to run along outside. Dat is when me notice di bumps all ova me body, or di way sometime me han an foot shake.

Di worst ting me do was to fall for Sed. Dat drive her crazy mad. She use to follow us about. Sneak roun di house when me in dere wid Sed. She took to she bed when Geno born. She get up when him loss. What a woman! When she die, me glad. Not because me want she dead, but becas di worl cause her so much pain. She need some peace. An so did I and I.

Me hear di sweet drum a talk.

Hyacinth, Clementina and Glory

"…Well, now you know bout her mother, bout her farder an her grandmodder, well, dat explain everyting. An dem seh she relate to dat woman name Lucretia."

"Lucretia?"

"Wah? You no know bout she? She famous roun dese parts. You know dat ole cow nearly bring we all down. You know dat? An di ole ones seh di same bout Lucretia. Nearly let Church go up in flame. One ole bitch deserve anodda. God forgive me, but wid people like dat as you hancestors, is no wonder she turn out how she did."

"You tink guilt follow you, Miss Hyacinth? You tink dat all we deeds write up in di great book of di Lord? Dat di book have likkle column wid ticks an scratch an numbers, dat mark guilt?"

"Miss Hyacinth? Miss Clementina?"

"Oh! Miss Glory! I didn't hear you."

"I said would you like more tea?"

"No, I wouldn't, but thank you kindly. Wait! Miss Glory, I wanted to tell you how sorry I am for you loss."

"Th…thank you and thank you for coming."

"I had to!"

"Miss Hyacinth?"

"Sorry, I didn't mean to shout. Dem heathen outside! Let me know if you want help wid dem. You should send fi Marshall. Di lack of respect is disgraceful. You have only to call pon me. Is not di firs time me save di town from dem badness. Well, mek me seh it plain, me and you modder didn't really see eye to eye."

"Yes, I know."

"I talk it straight. We could not stand each other."

"Yes, I know."

"But respec is everyting. And is me help her in she hour a need."

"What d'you mean?"

"I'm jus sayin."

"Sayin what, exactly?"

"Is me, is me tek her from di hangman noose!"

"What?"

"Yes is me, doin di work of di Lord!"

"I don't know what you're…"

"She neva tell you? Huh! Typical! You woulda been young. Was some trouble roun di harbour master. One day him garn. Jus like you bredda garn. Him was a nice man, white, but he marry him dark dark maid. People seh he was a holy terror and not a Christian. He was always nice to me. Well him garn, jus disappear one fine day. No one know where him deh and man from di mainland come down here, askin question, upsettin people, stopping trade. Tings get from bad to worse. People believe is she, yuh modder, have to do wid him disappearin. Y'know dey drag her outta here and tek her to di crossroads? Is me stop it. Stop it! I said. And, y'know, dey lissen me."

"No, I didn't know."

"No tanks is necessary. It was my neighbourly duty and God's work."

"I mus attend my other guests, Miss Hyacinth, Miss Clementina."

"Of course, of course."

"Nasty killin bitch, excuse my words, Miss Clementina. And dat poor boy… She never wanted dat poor chile; dat is why God see fit to tek him from her. To save him. And what kinda farder Mikey woulda mek – dat lazy, dutty heathen? Bout Black man is king and we all come from Africa! What a rubbish! Is mad him mad. I don't know nuttin bout Hafrica; me from right here. Smoke too much ah dat ganja, turn him fool. No wonder him modder die of shame – an him educate. If she was alive? Hah! Fire! She couldn't tek Seduce at all. It was she, she want Seduce fi swing. Me tink often, what a good job me go wid dem, dis funeral woulda been sooner."

"Is dat so?"

"Mikey's modder was a funny woman. She use to lurk roun dis house, mutterin an cursin, trying to juju di place, so her son would not go back dey, but him would just tek Seduce to di beach to do dem nastiness. Miss Clementina, yuh look puzzle. Yuh didn' know Mikey's modder?"

"No, Miss Hyacinth."

"What Mikey modder name was? Miss Celeste! How could me figet? Yes, Miss Celeste. No matter what she do, how she plead and beg Mikey, him always go back. Men so chupid. Seduce was always wearin hussy-paint an showin off she ancient titty dem. Me know me was just a little bit younger dan she, but to me she look like very old maggity mutton, dress as freshest lamb. She couldn't help herself. To me dat is di worse ting a woman can do. No pride, wotless. Some seh she tek wch me husban. But me not here to rake up nuttin. Dere was a time when we could not live good, me an she, and to not live good wid you neighbour is a sin, pure and simple. Me know me try, but we not here to judge, for dere is only one. An she dead and me is here…"

Seduce

A lie she ah tell! Lie! Green-yeye hog! Her time soon come, me ah wait fi she! You can do me anyting, but don't tell lie pan me! What an ole' nasty bitch tan bad! Dat harbour man? Filty beast. Bout him was Christian! What di fuckin raasclart dat got to do wid anyting? Dem is di worse! An she! Lie! Is a good job me dead! Mek me come back to tear out she goddamn troat, so she can't tell no more lie!

Mek me tell you how it go.

One day, Sally rush inna me hut. Glory sleepin. Sally brown an ugly – teet stick out. No one know how she manage to stay so fat, when sometime we so hungry. She have airs, tink she betta dan everybody becas she could read an write her name. It was big excitement wid her an she could chat, chat, chat wid nuttin to say. Di harbour master always call fi she to pass on him instruction. Some time she ac' like seh he was god himself. Ah fool, she fool.

…"Come, Sed, you have tings fi do. Di man ah call fi you."

"What man, me seh what man? Him not a man like everybody else? Him can't come to me? You nuh see me chile sleepin?"

"But listen to you mout, nuh! No Sed, him not like every man."

"Ah what di rahtid…"

She start fling off me clothes an fetch out some clean ones. She bustle roun me place like it belong to she.

"Come Sed, you ask too much question."

"Wait, what you doin?"

"Come nuh, Sed."

Me an she nearly fight. Mi box way she han.

"What is wrong wid you, Sally?"

"Sed, me jus come fram di harbour master office."

Me look her up an dung. "What's dat got to do wid me. Whatever you a give him ah fi you business."

She stop an sit dung. Di chair Mikey mek me start creak. Me wonder if dat is how di man feel. Under her. If dem creak so. She was richer dan all of us. Maybe di man like to creak.

"Ah tru, you no know."

"Know wah?"

"Sed, you nuh know di man..."

"Dem all di same."

"No, him one good man, generous. Dis could be you way out..."

I look pan her, an it come in like it was di firs time me really seein her. Big skirts fold roun her, her black an grey hair fallin out so patches of her scalp catch di afternoon sun from di window. Maybe she wasn't as well fed as me tink. Her eyes was begging, an her bottom lip ah trimble. Me get she meaning, but why me?

"Sally, you no do nuttin fi no one unless you ah get sumting, so stop goin roun di corner, come straight."

"Di harbour master ask fi you."

"So, mek him fine a nex one."

"No Sed, you nuh see it. How much longer do you tink dis goin las?"

"Wah you ah talk?"

"Dis, di alley, di life. You no see di town is growing and we shrinking. Soon dere won't be none of us left."

"Why is dat bad? You want to dead here?"

"No, but you know, people need fi eat, fi live. Dis is our way."

She start wring her likkle fat han in front of her.

"Di townspeople want us out. You tink when you leave here you goin get ah job, you goin in a shop, a school, di bank? No Sed, when you leave here, dere ain't nuttin else out dere fi you but ole age an death. Everybody know who we are, what we do. You tink a man goin come an marry you? Tek you weh? Wah?

Mikey modder goin give you she one son? No, Sed, dis is it, an we have fi hang on to it for as long as we can."

"Is what you want, Sally?"

"Dere's been a what is it... a partition. A piece ah paper dat everybody put down dem mark, or name if dem know how fi do it. Some say dey sending Marshall an his men to bun us out. Di harbour man seh he can fix it. But him want money an him want you."

"Wah? Why me?"

"Well, him see you, an him nuh know you."

Me haffi talk di troot, me was prideful, you know, and you know wah happen to prideful people. Dem get pull down. I was young an foolish. I did not know dat nuttin me do coulda change anyting.

"Me already sort out you pickney. One a dem gyal will have her. Come."

Me let her tek me outside and mek me wash in di cold barrel wata. She bring soap smellin of roses and lavender. She bring me back in and rub me down wid sweet almond oil, mix wid coconut. All di time she never stop talk.

"What, you nah big woman? You can handle him. Dem seh him can't use him ting no more – him wear it out! Dat no matter, is you him want. He will protec us, Sed, him go look afta us. Not even Marshall can do so much fi we. Come, you nuh know what an honour dis is. Yes, an honour. Him in a house Sed, tink of it, a house. An a bed, a big bed, wid sheet an pillow an mirrors..."

I could see di mist of me breath flow from me mout, on di glass me face press on. Me watch it grow an spread, like a gathering storm cloud, an den vanish back di way it come. Di glass crack an tiny branch dem reach out. Di hand dat hol down me head have a ring on it dat was cuttin inna me head. Di same as di han him was usin in me inside. All me could tink bout was di rings. What kinda rings? What shape, what size? What stone, what colour, what for? Rings of gold or silver? Wid small, small, small writing inside. Words a love an lastin? Not fi me.

Yes, indeed, dis was an honour.

Dat Harbour man give in to himself. Is not everyting you wish for you shoulda get. White man not in him country? Lef uncheck? Every thought an whim, bright wid di possibility of comin true? Lord God, di shame. It will mash dem. But you tek you ticket, y'hear? Eye fi yeye, teet fi teet, life fi fuckin life.

When him garn, every Lampi sing an dance! Why not? Was ah big feastin dat day. Even some ah di browns from di town come an celebrate wid us. Come in like someone tek we outta trap. Then mainlan man come down here, dey come to the Lampi sheds, bun down a couple, beat us, dem sure we know sumting. Which was fine wid di hypocrites dem, til it touch dem. Well, soon di good looks stop. Dem stop serve us in shops and mek we Lampis wait outside. Me already move back to di house up di hill, but dem fine me. Dem come bout four inna di marnin, di sun jus glimpse troo di trees roun di house. Didn't matta to dem dat dey lef me baby girl, cryin on di doorstep. Mikey's modder, Hyacint, Clementine modder, dat ole coolie bitch dat keep tellin people she Marshall auntie, an a few me nuh 'member.

Me scars itch, too much ah dem.

Me yeye swell, shut out di ugliness before me. What dem call it? Bloodlus? A lust fi blood, an is mine dem want and me shoulda draw it out me rarse an give dem! You see dat Hyacint dere? A bitch from Satan, mek me tell you. Nails scratch, teet bite an before me could tink straight dey was a rope roun me neck. Funny, it feel familiar to me. Me mine flash roun. Me goin let dem tek me? Not widout tekkin some a dem wid me. An believe me, me woulda tek anyone ah dem, bring dey arse before judgement wid me. Is Alfredo save some ah dem dat day.

Glory

This was always Mama's room. I found di Lord in dis room. Di las time I spend so much time in here I was close to death.

The duppies flew. They stood in corners whisperin an shoutin and whenever I came into the room dem stop what they doing – eating flowers an pieces of sky, singing songs only hearts could hear, dancing with longing for a place no longer home, making love under di tables, cooking food, chopping wood. Dem would turn an smile at me. Then rush to me an comb out my hair, wash me feet an tell me stories bout demselves. I could talk to them widout a sound coming from me mout and dey understood me betta dan anyone else. As a child I knew who they all were, but as a big woman me figet dem names. It was a secret I never tell. Me modder knew bout me and dem, but she never tell.

When me sheet wet wid perspiration, in the dark that feel like cushion pon me cheek, I call for dem. In truth, dey di real reason I wanted to come back from di mainlan. I missed them. Now my calls slap up flat against the darkness and slide to di floor. They do not answer, or cannot answer.

In dis room, di weight of the devil sit pan me. It sat on me ches'. I was fourteen or fifteen years. Jus di age when di devil like to play wid people, specially girl children. We ready to be play wid. This devil small an yellow an him tiny webbed hands close round me heart an lungs. He did not look at me, him watchin the duppies in the room, watchin Mama prepare di cinnamon oil she going to rub me down wid. She open the windows to let di devil out, but it have no intention of goin anywhere, an di duppies jus tease it, pullin its tail or pushing a horn. It jus sat on me ches an try to squeeze me life out. It waitin in di house long time for a soul to eat, fi tek a life. When di duppies find it outside, lying nex to di well, dem tek it in fi sport. Did things to it, stretch it out an almost make it feel pain. Dem ride it around the house. In return, fi vengeance, me tink it give dem memory an di desire to be around di livin. When we move back to di house, di whole place shake wid fear. What kinda people was we goin to be? When we move in, a ole man, wid one leg, but he still using the leg he couldn't see, help us carry our bags an ting, but Mama never see him. Dat is when me know me different, different from her, from she friends, from di other Lampi children dat I use to play wid. Di grips dem slip outta her han, but she did jus tink dem was too heavy. Me see him tek dem from her. He jus want him job back. Dem never came near her, dey jus watch her from afar, outta fear an love.

Mama burn leaves in the grate – they were meant to shoo away the ches' devil, but he seem to like it. Smilin down at me, relax and happy, wid his hands on my heart an lungs, squeezin an smilin. He waitin for di life to leave me, a life he would eat. Wid only di duppies for company all dese years, di devil was hungry. Mama move around, making the oil, making soup wid di herb Mama Pearl teach her how to use. Nothing in me body move cept me slowin heart, me emptyin lungs, an me eyes. Mama come to me an open me clothes. For one moment I thought she'd sold me for di highest price and that dey was a queue of men waitin to tear me apart. She rub me ches' wid di oil and whisper words that the past had given her. She rub hard. Di devil have a time holdin on. Di duppies stand around her, some greein wid what she doing, others shakin their heads an looking worried. She rub hard. Press all her fingers down an shift the tight skin one way and another, as if she fighting di skin self. The skin form small waves around she fingers and ripple out. She rub hard. She open windows an tek all di clothes off me. I start to shiver and she mek me drink di soup. I stare straight up and see in between di duppies a small spider crawlin over di ceiling, stopping sometime to worry about which direction it should take. Mama stay wid me, sleep in the chair beside me. The duppies watch us constantly.

"She nuh know what she a do."

"Every one know fi abate a fever yuh haffi open all di doors an windows an let in di fresh air."

"Close di doors an windows, man, she goin catch she death."

"Liquorice root."

"Frog tongue."

"A big black dog will scare dat likkle yellow devil."

"Likkle yellow brute!"

"Tek you han outta me fren!"

"Shall we kick it?"

"No, him grip go tighten."

I could only move me eyes as di duppies debate. Dem open an close windows an doors, fighting over di best remedy. Mama, sensing their presence, cuss dem away.

An then I remember, like a tiny hole of light boring in me head. I should pray. In school, which was di church on Sundays, we was learning bout Jesus and di Lord and dat he was our one true saviour. Mama use to laugh bout it. We never went to church, but me remember what di school teacher say. The Lord is our saviour. Surely, if I pray, he would answer? I prayed. No one hear, but I close my eyes and pray. I pray for all di badness Mama had done, I pray fo di papa me never see. I pray so close to me heart, like Jesus in di Garden of Getsemony, me sweat blood and me teet grind. I feel salt in me mout. And then a slap. Mama's open hand lef' a hot sting on my face. Was she slappin me cos me pray? Me tink so. She hit an hit. I try to slap her hands away but she push me down and sat on my stomach, kneelin pan me arms. And she kept hittin, til I felt no pain.

She rest and then say words; cook herb and mek more oil. She set a gourd full of stew by di tree and sprinkle rose water an brandy on di ground. Di devil smell the stew; di duppies dance before its eyes and show it di path outta me body an back to it own. He float off, an jus at the window he wink. I found di Lord dat day an all me duppy companion disappear.

I cried til me feel me heart goin burs'. Emptiness fill the gaps di duppies left. Is so long ago, so long. Did I imagine it? It couldn't have been real. The bible says... What is wrong wid people in this place? Obsess wid di dead. We see dem every-where, we talk to dem, pray to dem, talk about dem, mek up story bout dem. Di ole ways will be we downfall, like for dem heathens outside.

Seduce

Me member when it firs happen. Glory seh she did see a man, dat him look like a tree but move like a man. When she tell me dat, me know say it was me farder, come to look fi we. Lookin for Likkle Pearl, me tink.

Duppies so vain, selfish, like spoilt pickney. Me nuh understan di situation. I did not tink seh it goin to be some kind a duppy war. When we move inna di house, me an Glory jus' glad fi get way from di dirt road, di slack an mad neighbours. Me never imagine dat not only was di duppy warring wid me over di house, but dem warrin wid each other. One duppy want dis, next duppy want dat and di whole time Glory laughin at dem. She had di gift fi sure. She try to show me but me never did see dem, just hear dem and di blasted noise dat dem make. One time Glory seh a duppy tek a shine to me, seh how he know all about me reputation and he want fi come back and see me later. Me tell Glory to tell him go see Juicy Lucy instead. Me don't know if him did, she never say anything to me. But how would yuh know yuh sleeping wid duppy? Mine you, some people feel like dat anyway. Yuh see dat all di time. A lot a people dead before dey know. Yuh see dem, you can tell dat dem die long time. When Glory meet people for di first time she use to stare into dem face, just stare pan dem. I use to tink dat she saw sumtin I didn't, dat dey must have sumtin bout dem. Me never know and Glory never tell me.

Me an dis house always a fight. As soon as me walk in, me shout, "Lissen, dis is fimme house. You want fi live peaceful, den we can live peaceful, you want to fight, den come becas you time a run out." Dem accept Glory but not me. Me put sumtin one place, find it another. Dem try dem best to undo everyting me do. But me just carry on. Me stronger dan any a dem.

Another time, Glory sitting on the back porch, an she point and start laugh. She say di solja getting a backsiding from a likkle ole lady. Me tink dey come fi tell we dat it's dem dat really own di house. When dem get dey point across, dem leave. Glory wasn't di same for a long time after dat. Me tink dat is why she tek up wid dat wutliss sailor.

Me tink dat gyal love fi disappoint me. She love to grind me nose in it. She run weh wid dat dutty bwoy. You cyant tell me nuttin me nuh know bout sailors, believe me. She leave here for di mainlan – why dat godforsaken place me no know. Den him leave her. Nobody know what happen to him, him jus gwan. She come back to have Loo. Already have Son by den. Emerson, but we all call him Son. Me couldn't believe it. Me jus a mek porridge and sitting on my veranda when a horse and cart pull up. Out dem all jump. Son – him mussa been four or five – come running up. Me know it was him straight away. Me remember tink, trus she to have a bwoy. And den me see Glory. How she change! Get ole an ugly. It was over four years. She'd been suffering, but she never tell me. Casting her precious tings before swine. She was full full belly an sweatin to climb out di cart. Me never ask bout her business, an she never tell me, but me did tink she finally get up di strent to leave him. When she firs come back she look like frighten rabbit, always lookin roun her. She put me in mind of me modder. Di dutty bwoy never come fi dem. Me know him wouldn't; me jus know. And you know what she doin on di mainland? She a cleaner. A cleaner. Sometimes she make me feel sick. How could make baby after everyting me teach her. You know what she said to me, when me cuss? She tell me it was my fault. Mine. Me never tell she fi open her leg for di firs wotless, leggo-beast dat come long. Loo barn a few days late, like she ah wait fi come home.

Me couldn't really believe Glory have children. Me never tink any man would want her, too fraidy fraidy, like me modder. Me puzzle to know why she leave in di first place. Suppose was to get away from me. I did it to get away from

Pearl Before Swine. Even though she already dead, me still feel her displeasure. But yuh see, Big Pearl was right: all men are dogs. Glory mek dat big, shot-gun barrel, nose-hole sailor tek her away. Turn she into a fool – doh when me wave dem off, me did tink, tank di lord she grow up an livin she own life now. Me neva tink she would mek it dat far. When she lef school, she work roun di place wid me and when we couldn't stand each other no more, she go fi work in town, at di post office. In dem days only high yella people get work inna di banks an hospitals an schools. An dat was down to me. Me know what me doing when me choose her farder. Me tell her all di time. Yuh tink she grateful? Not a damn. She work inna di post office for years, never bettering herself. It break me heart to see she have no ambition. She was happy, I suppose, but yuh never could tell wid her. Me tink seh dat was dat, she not going to have children, den bam, dat jackarse turn she head and tek her away. Seems like di woman in me family always waitin to be tek somewhere else. Me never know woman foolish so. Me tell her, me warn her, see it deh. What she learn on di mainland? She learn how to keep she eyes to di ground. What did she learn to say? She learn to figet how to speak. She come back where people can see her. When she come back she old, older dan me

Dat Son fava him papa. But Lucretia! What a gyal. Me no tink Loo is Glory's own. Me tink seh dem spirits get togedda and swap roun. Playin jokes pan we, as is dem way. Loo full of di fire an ambition dat Glory don't have. Bright, loud. I never meet a child so loud. Fillin in di gaps her modder leave. Every move she mek, she mek noise, widout even opening her mout. An when she did open her mout she coulda barl. Me never like di barling – remine me too much of Likkle Pearl – so me tell her all she barling goin bring back di duppy wars, an she soon stop. You body have memories, y'know, even if dem not yours.

You don't have no idea what in Son head. Sometime he in di room an you figet him dere. But one time Glory seh she want fi leave an go back to di mainlan. Fi wah! I know seh she did feel dat Loo and Son didn't love her an she want to tek dem back. Loo always jus want me. Every time Glory pick her up, she barl an struggle fi come back to me. I know dem never want to leave. Son just stare in she face and tell her no, an run off into di bush. She want blame me fi dat, but dem pickney was home and dem know it. Glory fret, run round screamin, shoutin dat me put him up to it. Son never come back till she seh dem stayin. Stubborn. Him big eyes takin in everyting, givin nuttin back. Him still, like tree. Put me in mine of di story bout me farda. Dat bwoy use fi follow me roun, not talkin, jus following, him frog yeye pan me. Huh! But dem pickney did love me, better dan she.

... "Jesus upon the cross, who died for us, Miss Clementina, it is no surprise to me. Look at di whole family. Glory is di only Godfearin one. Me no know how she hasn't thrown herself unto di rocks arready. If me come from dem? God bless me, it would surely drive me mad wid grief."

"Troo word, Miss Hyacinth."

"Me see me boy, mek me speak wid him... Son... Son... Come speak wid yuh modder."

"A sad day, Miss Clementina. Mother?"

"Me know dis was goin to happen, you know why? Me have di gif. Mek me tell yuh."

"Yes, Mama?"

"I was tinkin bout me gif."

"Oh, Mother, I can't listen to your foolishness now, not today. You're supposed to be a woman of God!"

"Mock me if you wish, but I know what I know. An don't be fresh, son. I am a woman of God."

"I've heard you before..."

"Me know somting was goin happen, y'know why?"

"Mother... I have to..."

"Las week me did see a goat on di road, look like it was limpin, but di ting bout dis goat is dat it was on fire. Not big flames, jus a rollin fire under its skin. It was walkin toward me, an at first me couldn't mek out what was wrong wid its coat. Me stop an watch it walk slowly up di road, den when it come pass me, me see dat di coat was on fire."

"Dat is strange!"

"Yes, Miss Clementina. Me jus look; it walk pass me an it headin up di hill to dis very house. An di funny ting is dat it seem like a few people see it dat day in all part of town, so we know sumtin goin happen."

"Mother, I can't listen to any more of this nonsense. I'm going to tend to my flock, I'll speak to you later."

"Dat boy too higorant, Miss Clementina, don't mind him a reverend. But mek me tell yuh more. It was jus like di time Mass John, me husban, lef. Well, di night before, while I was washing di fish fi dinner, di fish head bite me an jump out di pan. Sweet Jesus dat died fi us, me couldn't believe it. It get weh down di road. I knew den dat sumtin was goin to happen. Me had to cook sumtin else. Mass John vex wid me. All we had was cornmeal porridge dat night. He didn't like it, but what can you do? In dose days you eat what you given. Dat night when Mass John roll off me – excuse me frankomen, Miss Clementina – him jus get up, didn't say a word to me, jus walk out di house an me never see him again. Dat was, let me see now, t'irty years ago. You see, God have a way of tellin us tings goin happen. Well she get she comeuppance now, for all dose marriage she mash up, for all dose lost souls dat she di wash outta she belly. So many, so many. She mus tek dat guilt to she grave."

Pastor Collins

God, my God, can you hear me? Listen to my mother! And I forbade the drums, but I can hear them from deep in the bush. Marshall will be called. To strike at his own people. Dry old spirit, with no love or life in him. What to do? I need to see her, like everybody else here; unlike anybody else, I know it's a sin to look. I know she's gone. I know they aren't listening, I know they will go to the bush tonight and try an find her. Heathens. Performing the devil's work. Yet part of me wants to go, wants to see her again, to say goodbye. But I'd be damning my soul and nothing is worth that.

The night she was passing, she sent Loo to tell me to come. I don't know what it is with that child but she unnerves me, she unnerves everybody. My wife would not have her in the house. My mother agreed. Her hypocrisy today – all solemn outside and happiness inside – makes me feel sick. She forced Loo to wait outside and I watched from the verandah, watched her talking an dancing to herself in the yard. There is no doubt the child is mad, but she's harmless. The arguments it caused whenever she came! Like a messenger from the devil, my wife say. She knew that when the call came, I'd have to go. I knew I'd be in this house for days, avoiding Glory, fighting old memories, fighting with her, working the provisions plot, an sleeping under the house bottom, like me use to.

One time Seduce send for me, me wife tell me if me go, she'd leave an take the children to her mother on the mainlan and I wouldn't see her or my children again. But I couldn't help myself. Then I had to go to the mainland and plead with her. Not good for the children. All the up an down. But I don't know why I didn't go this las' time. Aware of me wife behind the door, I ran Loo. Told her to go away, I wasn't coming any more. Now I feel shame. Maybe she call me to say goodbye. I'll always live with that regret.

But as I watch her neighbours, friends, enemies and her fellow old whores plotting to take over her final passing, I wonder why I'm here. Everyone is watching, waiting to see what I will do if the Lampis come for her. Will I fight for her soul or fight with God? They want blood, all of them. They want a bangarang, but the fight's already happenin in my heart.

I live the life Seduce wanted me to live. I marry like she want me to, even though, later, she say that was a mistake. I had children like she want me to. I became a pastor, like she want me to. But I can't reach her this time.

Glory is still watching me, after forty years she still watches me. The drums must be working on her nerves as well as mine. Her eyes grow big. She twitches like a bird. She thinks that somehow I took away her half-brother, Geno, but I never knew him. I was only a child. Seduce took me in to atone for her sins – all the babies she wash away in the river. I know that she was trying to appease a God she still fears, though maybe it was not God but her grandmother, Big Pearl Before Swine, or the Lucretia they all keep talking about. A slave who maimed and killed. How can anyone be proud of that? Seduce is the most respectful towards this mythical woman. Was she ever alive? People round here think so. Some think she was a devil woman who nearly destroy the island. Some see her as some kinda freedom fighter, like she really come to save we. I was almost jealous of her, this duppy from the past. Because of her influence on Seduce. People round here so desperate. If anybody get a reputation for anything, good or bad, them instantly related to them. It's pathetic. My wife even thinks she's related to the yellow-teeth Governor.

Mikey's still here, still mournin the relationship he shoulda had, mournin the son he lost. Mournin a woman that never really belong to him, never belong to anyone. That is what always bite Glory, her own mother never really belong to her, she had to share Seduce with everyone else. Let me speak to the old man. It's the least I can do.

"How are you, Uncle?"

"Pastor Collins, tank yuh for you kind words."

"I'm sorry for your loss. I know how much she meant to you, how much you meant to each other."

"When a man has a love fi a woman and she has love fi him, it is ordained by the most high dat who him put togedda, no man can pull asunder."

"How are you in yourself?"

"All is well. I and I soon joining her."

"Don't say that. I know you're grieving."

"More dan you can imagine."

"I, I, can imagine..."

"I an I neva know a woman so difficult."

"But you still have your life, your health..."

"But me lose me heart. She fight against I love."

"Yes, I mean..."

"She couldn't settle in her mine, you understan? Her spirit haunted. Even when me tell her, no badda wid di man dem, me coulda provide fi we both, she wouldn't lissen."

"Maybe that is how she took care of..."

"I an I coulda tek care of her, me tell you! She... she... Is not an easy ting to share di ting you hol' mos dear to you heart..."

Mikey

... When I and I look at her me remember how me couldn't keep away even when she treat me like shit. When Geno born she keep him from me. I hide, under di window of di shack on di alley. Sed been at her granny house for a while, but every now an den, when she short a money, she come back into town. An so, I and I hide like a common tief. When I dare to glance up through di window me see Geno, jus born, asleep on some rags in di corner. Glory was on di pallet. Seduce had lifted up her skirts into a bundle in front of her and she squattin over some man. Me couldn't see him face, jus di top of him sweatin, baldin head. Sed have she eyes close. Me knew dat face so well. I know she tryin not to feel.

"Easy, gyal, you goin bruk me wood."

"Shut you mout, man, time is money... Kiss me neck, bwoy!"

He start to groan and his noise could be heard all along di alley, an me know straight who it was. Chesta. Everybody know Chesta buck like a mule an squeal like a pig. Most of di odda Lampis would not touch him. Di squealin put dem off. I sat back down under di window. It was not di firs time I had seen her fucking someone else, but still it feel like me heart goin stop. Di groans grow. Chesta squeal.

"Can't you shut up you mout!" I hear Seduce getting vex.

"Oh Gad, oh Jesus Lord, eeeeee, eeeee, eee!"

Chester squeal him final squeal, pantin, whinin into di bed. Seduce continue to rock to her own riddim. Chesta look at her; him look scared. Perhaps he saw dat she no longer wid him but wid someone else. He stare until she gasp, throw back her head an let out a long, slow sigh. Di hair raise up at di back of me neck.

Chesta pick up him clothes, an as him put dem on, him eye she up an down.

"You carry on like seh nobody in di world matters, cept you."

Seduce was ova a bowl of wata, washin herself. "You want love, go sleep wid you bull-cow wife; you want satisfaction, come to me."

"You cyant talk bout me wife like dat!"

"An wah? Is weh you goin do?"

"You mean to seh dat you don't feel nuttin fi me?"

"Chesta, gimme me money. What you expec, dat di sight of you greyback self goin sen me crazy? *You* crazy. Feel wha? Chu, you all di same."

"Alright den, halright." Chesta, upset, slap down he money on di bed. "I'm nat comin back!"

"Good! You mek too much noise."

"Is who yuh a talk so? Me? Mek noise? Now who is crazy?"

"Chesta, you know what me an di odda Lampis call you? Squealin Chesta, becas you soun like a pig!" She laugh after him as him slam di door. He was outside, fixin himself, cussin under him breath, an den him see me. Me no give him no time to reac, me jus tek up a piece of ole firewood, still smokin, an tomp him on di side of him face wid it. He fall to di groun moanin. It disgust me, turn me stomach. Many times when I and I been wid her, an Glory sleepin in her cot, by di bed, me neva tink nuttin bout it. But dat man an Sed, wid me chile in di room, I and I just want to kill him.

"Squeal sumtin for me now, Chesta, man." Me stan ova him an clap him again. Me see teet fling out from him head, an him roll ova. Me hol up di stick to box him again, an his blood an spittle drippin down di piece a stick in me han. It was feelin di warm blood on me dat stop me deliverin di next blow. Him groanin, try fi stan up an me plant me foot inna him backside. Dat seem to move him. He look up an see me, fraid, an start fi scramble up. Dat is what dem times was like. Black life cheap, cheap, cheap. Nobody woulda done nuttin to me if me cut him wid di knife inna me pocket, an dem go fine him in one corner a town, dogs feedin off a him. Who would a miss him, di gutter rat, who would a fight fi know wha happen to him? No one.

"Wah, Chesta, where yuh goin, yuh tink yuh get yuh money wort?" I start to fling any stone me can fine after him. Me turn roun to look back at di shack. Seduce was outside, lookin at di whole ting. She never say a word.

"Look!" Me fling di stick after Chesta. "Look!" – showin her me blood-soak hands – "Look wah you mek me do. Dis is yuh." It look like she smilin. She jus turn roun an shut di door. Me feel like she wanted me to hang fi her.

Me is a man dat no have no control. Control over what? Everyting have to go her way. Jus like me modder. Everyting. When me leave fi di Black Isle after Geno loss, me tink me never goin see her again. Dey is only so much time you can let you heart be broken. When me get back to Church it come in like it was nuttin. Me an she fall back into how we always was. She never ask me how me do, what it like on di Black Isle. She just knew me was comin back. I and I hate dat. One night, in di house, sittin pan di veranda, me seh, "You love me?"

"No."

"You lay inna you bed, tinkin bout me?"

"Damn arse!"

"You dream bout me?"

"What for, you here don't it?"

"Dat is not what me a seh."

"But we is old. Me is not some love-struck chile."

"No, lissen me."

"Lissen di crickets singing."

"Lissen me nuh. Is you why me come back."

"A lie you a tell. You bruk an no want to die inna foreign."

Me jump up from di veranda an walk back di six miles to town, in di darkness. It was black, black, black. Back den everyting darker dan now. No cars pan di road, everyting candlelight an kerosene lamp. Nuff house burn down back den. So me walk into town, cussin all di way. Me go straight to Paradise an knock at her ole door and feel surprise dat she not dere. She gone. Get her own way, again. Selfish.

Maybe she goin to buck up pan me modder. Dat will be one

hell of a fight. Me hear di tonder-clap over yonder mountains. Maybe dats dem. Sizing each other up, lookin fi weaknesses.

Both a dem had a firm grip on mine.

Seduce neva really give me di idea she want me or me babies, after all dose times, all dose years. Then Geno. Outta no where. Geno. Me modder tink Sed get pregnant on purpose, just to keep me. An den she tink she get rid of di chile to spite her. Me no know. Geno. Him born wid him eyes open, on a Friday. Di ole ones seh sumting bout dat. Him look like one of di firs ones, one a di firs people dem. Never before me feel like how me feel fi him, like me no know. Like if smady arks me, me dead fi him. Me cyant find di words. Jus like dat, me dead fi him, him mean dat much to me. When him gone, me no know what happen to me. Like smady come an chop off me han, me foot, an tear out me heart at di same time. Jah! I and I love him more dan her, for in him beat I heart. Tink she did know dat. Fimme prince. Like all men, me no know woman at all, at all. No know woman a damn. Woman practice dem magic pon we. We no know. We neva know. Back in dem days, a pickney could jus show up at you table an dem yours. Dey was no colonial trackin, no papers to prove who dem is. Some people jus tek people pickney, some give dem away. If you no have no money and you have relative dat cyant have dem, you give dem one a yours. Dat's how it was in dem days. You tink it's some likkle pickney dem fine inna bush? A nation of loss children lookin for home. How me nuh know dat she nuh kill him? Me know seh she have di skill. How me nuh know dat she jus lef him, jus to get back at me for bein a man? Is weh him go? How can you lose a chile inna you own house? Is weh him go, who tek him? Dese are di questions dat nearly kill I dead, why I and I had to go to Black Isle.

Five years, me gone, five years. She not even ask me if me reach Black Isle. Well, me did reach. Me get dere quick, quick, quick. It was comin back dat took so long. Me shock how much me miss Church. When me lan pan di Black Isle everyting was suppose to be fi di Black man. Dis was di firs lan we own, but di place see too much of its people die, ravage by war an hunger, disease an sumtin me cyant put my finga pon, sumtin like disappointment, like di lan disappoint in we, an di whites tryin to tek it back all di time. Dere was no let up, no pause fi tink, jus fightin. Me kill me firs black man ova dere. Me tink me was goin to hang for sure, but no one come, no one mention it. Di lan was hard like di people, like stone. Everyting was dus an dirt, no fertile soil, everyting get suck outta di place. Dem sen out di call for Black brothers, a call to arms fi help defend what was ours, but when me get dere, dere was nuttin to defend, bare rock an dry stony earth. What me leave home for? Sed tink she di only one dat feel. Di only one dat know dat. When me lose me son me lose me mine. I and I went to di Black Isle to die. Instead me fine meself, me fine love, di love of a good woman an me tink me didn't miss Sed at all.

I an I love dis woman straight away. It was sumtin about her eyes, her face. Like a still wata me could dive into. Isatou. She love me so much. Not like Sed. Seduce was steel, Isatou was cloud. Even when we togedder, you feel like Seduce jus put up wid you. But Isatou would do anyting fi me, she woulda die fi me. Dat is love an me lef her an her children we have togedder. I was hurtin still. I couldn't be a farder to dem becas di one me want tek weh from me. Her language was that of some of the sailors me know, di ones wid dark curly hair an dark, dark blue-black skin. Isatou. Den when me seh how me plannin to come back, she fall pregnant. It come in like Jah ah give me anodda chance. But she sickly. No matta how much tea an juice an good food me mek her, she lose it an me couldn't look pan she. Me feelins tek ova. I an I blame her an treat she like nuttin. One marnin she garn an I relieve, Jah know, for I and I had not di courage to leave.

Sed knew. When me come back she could tell.

Pastor Collins

I'm returned to a time I'd all but forgotten, more than forty years ago. I've no idea how I got there. I hardly remember how long I was in the bush, but I remember the first time I saw her, not knowing if she was a river spirit or a devil. It was Seduce, crouching over the river. The water moved her skirts behind her. When I ran away, it was always to the river, trying to get away from my mother. Seduce was washing herself. I must've been five or six. I don't remember why I'd run away. I see the back of her, big broad shoulders, thick black plait that fell down her back and her skin the colour of shadows. I know she heard me; her back stiffened an she slowly turn to look at me. There I was, small, dark, skinny, skinny, skinny, belly bloat out, with a mass of white hair. I can't remember a time my hair wasn't white. She just look at me for a long time. I know that I did feel tired and lonely but not scared of her, only wary. My mother had told me to keep away, that she ate children, but even then, as a child, I knew Mama was lying. She held out her hand and I just took it. I can still feel the touch of her hand, wet from the river, holding on to mine, as she led me through the bush back to the house. Glory did not speak to me. She looked fraid of me white head. Seduce took me to the kitchen that seem to me the size of the whole house. It had a fire, as big as a doorway, in one wall, an a long table in the middle. It hasn't changed, still the same, just the fireplace stands cold. Seduce tried to make me sit down but I hid under the table. She tried to coax me out. She gave me some chicken soup. All under the table. She gave me food, a pillow an a blanket, an then she leave me. And that is where I stay, don't remember nothing before it or as sharp after.

Sometimes she washed me, try to comb me head, but it was too knot up. She ask for why my hair was white. What had I seen? Me see nuttin, me say, an she say that was enough. She shave me head and burn the hair and bury the ashes out in the bush by the house.

Mama would come screaming to the house to tell Seduce to let go of me. Sed would send me back, with new clothes. My mother would tear them off and burn them. But I would find myself back there.

Why Glory thinks I have anything to do with Geno going, I don't know. I start coming to the house some years after he'd gone. He would have been a little older than me. I think that is why Seduce took pity on me. She never try to dash me from under the table, she just left me food an go. It was easy for me an Glory not to talk to each other. Glory hated me an I hated her. I can barely stand her now. My wife says Gloria thinks she's too good. That is true, that was always true.

Seduce told my mother to send me to the seminary on the mainland. Mama didn't want anything from her, not even advice, but somehow she sent me. I think Seduce helped her and I dread to think how she paid for it. Laughable, really, that a man of the cloth gets put through school by such means. Now I have my own church and a house next to it, though my wife never wanted to come here. She thinks that Seduce an Glory, an even Loo, tryin to bring us down, that they don't like me to do well. She fraid of them, she think that the men of the family never survive, that any man who goes near them, they kill them or lose them. That is why Son leave. I think that is why Seduce sent me away. It broke my little heart. I never really forgave her for that. I didn't hear from her for years.

The school was run by missionaries from Europe, sent to tame the region. For some reason, which is now obvious to me, they never came to Church, but stayed on the mainland. They told us that Church would sink into oblivion with the weight of sin and evil that resided here. They kept my past from me so I started a new life, the old forgotten. I was young and eager to please. I became a man of religion, opposed to her lifestyle. She broke off from me. She said I had forgotten myself. I said I only had to remember the Lord. She wanted me to rise to prominence in the church, become a bishop. I did rise, but then I brought my wife and children with me, telling my wife it was the Lord's work to come to this place. But it was she I wanted to see. When we entered the house she looked us up an down. It reminded me of the look she give me at the river all those years ago. Seduce said she didn't like my wife, that her spirit was sour, her blood couldn't take to her. My wife say to look at Seduce turn her stomach, such was the badness in her. Mama was grateful. For years she'd lived on my reputation, her big son on the mainland, and now I was home, the living proof.

When we came back, I remember how Glory gave me a shallow half hug, the kind designed to keep someone away, not draw them close. We prayed together, for she had found the Lord, much to Seduce's disgust because it wasn't her Lord.

All now I catch Mikey looking hard hard at me. What's for him now, with no Seduce to fight over?

What to do? I owe her my life, an yet the life she wanted for me tells me she is wrong. I begged my wife to have the dress made for her. That was a mistake. I wish I hadn't now. To the devil with respectable! Seduce would have hated that colour an somehow my wife knew. Then it was too late to fix, but I had to give her something. I asked Glory if she could wear it. I think Glory was happy to put her in something decent. Seduce was not a decent woman and I loved her for the whole of my life.

Glory

What a holy show he's putting on, what a holy show. He musta spit pan everybody in di place. Spitting his lies and holy righteousness. Troot is, him no righteous. Just a liar and a tief. No one knows dat except me. His head always white, sitting on a youthful face. What a way him rock an turn?

I don't know when him start come roun. Hyacinth use to seh she pregnant all di time. Mama used to say she dry up and lie, but sure enough, one day she pass by, which was hard to do cos we way up di hill, and tell us she goin away to have she baby at her modder's place, ova di mountain. We all surprise. Her man gone long time, but Mama say it was neva a surprise to see what man would lay wid. She come back after. I don't really know how long, and there he was. Doe-eyed and white haired. Coming to jus sit under di house bottom.

He took it, you know, he took it all. Di more me give him, a di more him take. I'd knock over his bowl of water, so he'd have to fetch some more from di well outside. I'd fill his food wid ashes, draw his plate on the ground and spit in it. An he would eat it, his eyes fix on mine, one slow mouthful after di other. One time Seduce jus happen to glance at his plate. She saw di mess in there and snatch it away from him.

"Eat it!" She shove it under my nose and wait for me to say no. "Eat it!"

Don't know what was going through my mine. Fear catch me, but me tink me could fool her.

"Is alright, Mama, me have me plate right here," an I start stuff me mout. It was fry fish an green banana. She box it out me han, grab my chin an squeeze open me mout til she shook di food outta me.

"Me seh eat it." You know what dat boy do? Seeing me start fi cry he snatch it out a Mama han an start to eat it. She knock it from his han, but then he fell to di floor and ate up everyting, quickly, almost making himself choke. Seeing dat jus make me hate him all the more. He wasn't doing it for me, he was doing it for her. He ran out di kitchen an hid under di house. Dat's where he always went when he was scared. She look at me and I did think I was going to get di biggest backsiding of me life. But I was wrong. She tip out her plate, next to mine on di floor, and stand in it. Stamp her foot an work it into the dirt floor.

"Eat it!"

I cried and cried, "Mama, no, is di boy, di boy..."

"Eat it!"

I try to run but I couldn't. She grab me and press me to the floor. Wid one han gripsing me neck, wid di other she beat me in my back. She force me face close to di ground. I ate. Coughing, choking, barling, I ate. I don't know how long she held me, don't know, until all the food was gone. I saw his eye looking up through the floorboards at me. He saw my humiliation. Eyes lock unto mine. I know him smiling up at me. I coulda died. When me finish she push me over. I was a mess, spit and vomit over me clothes. As a final blow I could hear her coaxing dat devil pickney out from under di house. She lead him to her bed an lay down wid him. As I lay in ashes and dirt and vomit, me hear she sing him to sleep. Not long after dat she sen him away, an she hate me for it ever since.

Alfredo, Pastor Collins, Mikey and Clementina

"Sorry, sorry, I don't mean to... ahm... interrupt."

"No, no, we were just talkin."

"How are you, Pastor Collins?"

"Oh, fine, fine. I see we are having another christening."

"Yes, Pastor, my youngest. My wife feel he will be denied the kingdom of heaven if we do not christen his two-month ol' self. What d'you think?"

"We are all welcome in the kingdom of God."

"Dat is what me tell she."

"Ha, Alfredo, you never change. Excuse me, perhaps I can leave you to look after Mikey here..."

"You need lookin afta, sir?"

"I will tek some rum, if that's what you mean. How are you, postman? How is your brood?"

"Oh, fine, fine, you know."

"No, I don't. I and I was never blessed wid children. How much you have?"

"Seven."

"God said go forth and replenish the earth. You done wid replenishin it yet?"

"Haha, yes sir, me tink me done."

"What are you doin here?"

"Wha?"

"Come, what you doin here?"

"I had to come."

"Oh, but you wife not happy bout it."

"No, but a man cyant be rule by woman all his life, heheh."

"I was thinkin bout dat."

"How you holdin up?"
"Look out, she ah come."
"Huh? Who?"
"Alfredo! What are you doin?"
"I'm talkin to… to…"
"Don't you know he is one ah dem dutty filthy madman!"
"Clementine, that's rude!"
"Alfredo!"
"Go! Look Glory is servin tea. Gwaan nuh."
"But I…"
"Go!"
"Well…"
"Me sorry bout me wife, sometime her brownness can lead to ah lack ah manners."
"Dat is di way of dem people – upperty. No need, postman, me know. You have you own tings you tinkin bout?"
"I've… ahm… been meaning to talk to you. Well, can… ahm… we talk?"
"Come mek we sit on the veranda and reason."

"Good evening, ladies."
"Peace an love to you."
"Alfredo, Mikey, you come fi fine we?"
"No, sisters, me an Alfredo goin talk, tek in a likkle air."
"Oh!"
"Put down di knife, sistren, dem nah do nuttin."
"Peace, ladies, peace, we nuh trouble you."
"Postman! You come fi stop us?"
"No, no. Me jus talkin to Uncle here."
"Cos you blood is as good as any one's"
"You flesh sof'."
"Gentle, gentle."
"We will go roun so, out di way."
"Keep it dat way."
"Yes."

"Dey expectin trouble, postman."
"Are you?"

"Trouble go always find my Sed. Now what d'you want to talk to me about?"

"You 'member the bangarang, no not di big bangarang but di trouble over di harbour master? No, you weren't here and I had to help."

"What you talkin bout?"

"I've never told this to anyone. Well, di harbour man was out of control, a white man garn, how dem seh, native?"

"Dat is not native, dat is white man uncheck, but me know who you mean."

"Well, him runnin di harbour like him own personal kingdom. He make ships pay nuff to dock here and he make us pay to get the goods. It was crippling us."

"Yes, I and I know."

"He was squeezing di life outta us."

"So what di people do?"

"Oh, have secret meetin, send lettah to di governor, send lettah to di mainland – foolishness dat got us nowhere."

"You shoulda organise."

"Yes, but we..."

"Fraid?"

"Then one day him disappear. It turn out dat he was di son of smady important on di mainlan. Dey sen men to look fi him and dem was tearin up di town. No one slept. Everyone feelins was fever, desperate fi tings to go back to normal. We all ah blame we neighbour, fearin names would be named. But he was not found and someone had to be blamed. Seduce. It turn out dat as well as hurtin di business in town, di man was a terror to di Lampis.

"Dey drag her to the crossroads, outside of town, to di tree we all know an fear. It wasn't Marshall and his men but di women of di town. A mass of women, screamin, yellin in a frenzy like you've never seen before. Dem stop bein human, dem was all animal. Dem decide dat it musta been she, and in dere wisdom dat dey was judge, jury and executioner. I was on my horse, mekkin my deliveries, newly in the job of postman. I'd only recently got dat horse – I use to have a donkey. If we was still pan dat ole slow, miserable donkey, mebbe di two of we dead. I came upon dem. Women held her either side. Dem pull at the rope dat hold her hans behine her back, anotha rope was roun she neck. Her face was bloody, her breas' expose; one had teet marks."

" 'Kill di bitch!'

" 'Mek she suffer!'

" 'Sen she back to hell!'

" 'Is she kill him.'

" 'Whore a Satan!'

" 'Jus like her people, murderers an tief, all a dem!'

" 'Dem goin sen militia fi sure.'

" 'We town ruin, cos of you!' Dat was Hyacinth. She mek a swing afta her and box her in di jaw. She mek no soun. Me spirit couldn't stand what was happenin; it hurt me to see her treated so.

" 'What is goin on here?' Come een like my shout startle dem, dey all start shouting.

" 'Stay outta dis! Is nuttin to do wid you.' I didn't know she den but dat was you modder. She wipe blood from her mouth.

" 'Move yuself!'

" 'We have to do sumting!'

" 'Dis bitch send us to we death!'

" 'Di town goin perish.'

" 'Yes! Galang! Is woman business.'

"I said, 'What is goin on?' I dismount an stride towards dem, no idea what me was goin do. 'What are you goin to do to dat woman?'

" 'Do you know who she is?'

"For a moment, everything stop. Dem all look at me. I look at her, her eye keepin mine. 'No, I don't know her.'

" 'You lie!' Hyacinth stoop down and pick up a rock. She intended to throw it afta me.

" 'I tell you, I don't know her. And may I remine you, marm, dat I am a government worker, goin about my work. Trow dat rock an you will be in big trouble.'

"Anotha woman grab she han an mek her dash down di rock.

" 'Who is she?'

" 'Di biggest whore pan di island.'

" 'I can assure you marm, she not di only one.'

" 'She is di cause of all dis trouble.'

" 'You mus know bout di harbour man. Well we tink is she dat get rid of him.'

" 'She kill him, dat is all she people good fa!'

" 'But how d'you know? What does Marshall say? Where is he?'

" 'Someone gone get him, but him won't do nuttin; she's his whore too.'

" 'Dem man, dey wreckin di town.'

"' Tearin down we homes, businesses, everyting we work fa.'

" 'An today, dem fine him clothes, wid blood pan dem, near di Lampi sheds.'

" 'Dat don't prove she did it.'

" 'Man, look out! You look like a fool and we got no time.'

" 'We goin deal wid it. No one else will. If we show di mainlan dat we mean business, dat we deal wid it ourselves, they'll leave we alone.'

" 'Yes!"

"She seh nuttin, stare ahead of her like she seein nuttin, hearin nuttin. Di sun high, heat made di road dance, di horse jittery an sweat pour outa everyone.

" 'Lissen, you not from here; you don't know.'

" 'I don't know, but I know dat dis gainst di law.' I inched forward, I had to get her away. 'Dat if we cyant behave like law-abiding citizens den we all lose. You tink you doin di right ting? Buckra will use dis to hold we back. Dey will claim we can never govern weselves.' I tek a hold of her. She stand in front of me, di ropes on her hands mekkin her fingers blue.

" 'Come,' I said, 'if you believe in God, you mus believe in justice.' I took di ropes from Mikey's modder. Mentioning di church stop dem in dem tracks.

" 'What would di priests seh? Are you God?'

"I pushed her forward. She fell and I pick her up and lift her onto my horse.

" 'I'll tek her to town. We'll be dere before you reach you yards an cook you man food.' Di horse rear, di women cower.

'Go home. No one need to know bout dis. Justice will be done.'

"I back di horse away as me talk, and den I turn an ride from dem as fas as me could. I hear shoutin but I dare not stop to see. My, dat horse was fas' yu'know! White foam gather round him neck. Wid her arms roun me, I press dat horse further, faster dan it had gone before. When I look back dey were still dere, getting smaller, one body, many arms an leg an eye, all lookin afta we."

"You know, she never tell me."

"I wasn't sure..."

"Not a word. Then what?"

... Me rememba a slow drop of sweat sit on she forehead just up from di black eye dat swallow you whole. I look pan dat drop of sweat til me could see me own desire in it. Me could see me own face, me eyes, hungry and desperate, me mout dry an empty, waitin and wantin her. She? Sweat for me? Me nuh tink so. Me tink di sweat a follow him own mine, follow me heart an fine him way closer to she dan ever me could. She a sweat bout me? No. She a sweat fi sheself.

She sweat pour pan me like sweet almond oil, honey an rosewater and rub and rub til me skin remember its name an pledge allegiance to me. Dat bead of sweat on she forehead neva move, neva shake. Me tink it pon she like jewel on di head of an Indian goddess.

Me buy me economic freedom and me domestic captivity by wooing di brown daughter of the brown post master, but it was always Seduce dat have me heart.

That night we rode through di cane. Blacka feel me heel. It was di firs time she hang pan me, di firs an di las. Me can still feel she breath pan me neckback as we rode an rode, di cane partin like a woman bout to deliver. Cane have it own song you know, so me farder tell me. Is we who figet to listen, doh by di state of him han, di look of him back and di brokenness dat live in him eye, me neva want to hear dat deh song. Me tink me hear it dat night. We knew as we rode, and she hang on, dat we condemning di watchman to big trubble, even a beatin. You see, once parted, di cane don't come back just so. You can tell sumting been troo dere. Di cane contain di shape of a man, a woman an a horse. Me feel blood seeping out me parts. Di wind whipping di cane all over us. When we reach Claremont Hill we dismount. As me help she down, she took me…

"Well, she get off my horse, I don't know where exactly and me jus tink she go home."

"She neva tell me. What a woman, what a mystery!"

"Yes sah."

… She took me. Took me. Is not always man tek woman, you know. She know it an feel it an she smell rub itself with mine and the horse and she took me. She take me to the valley where di mountains protec di pasture, she open me and let the wind and earth an stars fall in. Me heart find itself in me mout. She cover me wid herself as she press us togedda and I listen to my brain and hunger pop. An all you could hear was the sound of di cane. Is what she did. When she finish, she seh, "Payment", and walk off into di bush.

Me could not leave her, could not leave her even doh I could lose everyting. Me wife, di pickney dem, me station in life. Me watch me farder die in di arms of him second wife, longing for di first. He die of grief and give me all di money his pain and sufferation brought him. An Clementina young an pretty den, wid clear skin and good teet, when she mama give her to me. Dem spoil dem pass-for-white daughter – till she open she mout and den you knew she pure Church. Dem save her, not fi a white man but not fi a black one needa. Always in a hat to shield di sun from bring out she true colour. But when she smile, her eyes down, me tink of another. An when she peel off her clothes – dem days long gone – like a ripe banana, me tink of another. An even when she tek me where mountain air breathe through you skin, and di sun shine at the base of you heart, when she lay crying, and me and she not knowing dat already our first child was forming, I did think of another.

Di Lampis too black fi di whites and browns, too bold and knowing fi di church. Dem form dem own government and Seduce was di head. An she took me to where light an dark ran into each other before fallin away.

We had let the cane tear at us, so we could tear at each other. I member dat sweat, glistening in the moon, when she turn away from me, into di bush.

Seduce

Me was never a gyal. Went from baby to woman in a blink of an eye. It was how me mek. Mama Pearl saw it, which is why she start cuss me from marning.

..."Me tell you how you mek, gyal?"

"Yes, Mama."

"Me tell you de depth of degradation reach for your conceiving? Answer me!"

"Yes, Mama."

"Dere has never been such a person, such a gyal as you. Memba dat. You is filth and debasement. It was di filth kill off you modder and it go kill you."

"Yes, Mama."

"Fine di Lord, fine di Lord, fine di Lord."

"God? What God know? Him a man. What man know? If dem seh, fi hundreds and thousands of years, God white, den you ah pray to a white man? See ya, Ma! You give me too much joke."

"Me give you joke, Seduce?"

"No, Mama."

"Yuh don't want to lissen! Filth clog up you ears! Go get di switch!"

An she beat me, beat me, beat me, til sweat flow from us both, she beat me til she feel like buckra. Every now and den she let the sun warm she back, den she go on beatin.

"D'you believe in God?"

"Yes." So me seh. Yes me believe dat him is a sonofabitch and when me catch him, me goin twist off his beard.

"Do you believe in di son, di farder an di holy ghost?"

I believe in di moon, di womb and di blood dat connect me to the sky.

Big Pearl Before Swine seh Likkle Pearl was delicate, small. She snap in two if you hug her. She seh one day a tree, she had never seen dat kind before, jus appear in di yard, on di opposite side to di coffin tree. Big Pearl seh she try to chop it down, but di machete never connect to di wood. It come in like it move out di way. She seh she scratch off a piece a bark, she seh it bleed, but she hear no noise. Soon dem jus lef it. Likkle Pearl was no less dan ten, no more dan fourteen. She fine herself drawn to di tree. Every opportunity she have to sit under it she would. As she grow, so di tree grow. Big Pearl say it was waitin, waitin fi Likkle Pearl's first signs of womanhood.

Dis is what Likkle Pearl tell Big Pearl before Swine an dis is what Big Pearl tell me.

Likkle Pearl was jus below di house, plantin cassava when she look up. She never see anybody but dey was di smell of smoke, like burning sugar cane. She feel the touch of sumtin like a warm breeze cross she neck, like smady breath. Dat night she could not wait to fall asleep so dat in di morning she could rush out in to di yard an get dat feelin again. She stand outside all day. Come evening, Big Mama Pearl Before Swine beat her wid her stick fi mek her come in.

Di breaths came an went. Den came di touches, caresses so slight it feel like it jus you skin ripplin on its own. She never did see anybody. Day in, day out di seduction take place. You see, a so me name. She seh it was many months. Di hint, di suggestion, di touch so soft you wonder if you feelin dem at all. She start to feel dat di world was only a dream, an what was happenin to her was real. She start to run a fever an nobody know what wrong wid her. She want sumtin bad, bad, bad, but did not know what she want. Is him she did want. Dat want for a man can drive a woman to madness. All di wanting mek her sick; yuh body can only tek so much. If you don't give it what it want, it turn pan you. She couldn't tek it no more, an one night everybody tink she goin dead, an dem call a preacher. Big Pearl say she was sweatin, talkin in tongues, screamin, cryin, growlin like a wild ting from outta bush. She have to be tied to di bed. Dis went on fi some days. Big Pearl stand ova her day an night, jus talkin, talkin, talkin, prayin, prayin, prayin to her. Di preacher seh dere was nuttin to be done, an him leave. Big Pearl need some res so she go an lay down, an warn Theotis, she yard man, to stay watchful. Theotis seh dat him nearly sleep nuff times, but it was only rum dat keep him goin, as him sit in a chair near she bed. Theotis seh dat he was only dere a few hours when di rags holding her jus fell away, an she jump up an throw sheself through di window. Him shout, "Madam, Madam!" but it too late. By di light of a low yellow moon, Big Pearl see Likkle Pearl run into di yard, and den she run, run out into di bush.

People say she dead, or so chupid she loss an don't know her way back home. Big Pearl never believe dat, know she alive but did not know when she go see her again. Many weeks later Likkle Pearl stumble back to di house an collapse in di yard. She was confuse, cover in bruises, bite mark, scratches an dirt. It leff her mad, lost to us an never to return.

Dis is what Big Pearl get out of her as she was beatin her.

Likkle Pearl find herself in a clearin deep in di bush an did not know how she get dere. Di big yellow moon cast shadows dat she could not distinguish. A tree tek its branch an wrap her up in dem. She could feel di same breath as before, di branch an twig slowly slowly inchin roun her, keepin her. She say she pass out an den wake up an fine sheself still dere. Di moon leave to be replace by a weak sun an den di moon come back. She stay like dis, wantin to move, not wantin to move. One cold night, suddenly di pain an pleasure stop. But she could not believe it, an wait an wait in exactly di same spot, di same position. She realise it not coming back an put she legs down and crawl back to di house.

No one believe her, cept Big Pearl, who jus fall down prayin. Big Pearl try fi get rid of me; I was di proof of her daughta degradation. Likkle Pearl seh she could hear me laughin when me still in she belly. Big Pearl give me modder all manner a tings fi tek, chew di bark of a certain tree, boil up bush to drink, bart in oils dat mek her sick, but nuttin work; it was already too late. I had already come to be. Some people tink it was duppy dat sire me, we bad blood come back to tek us. Some say it was one a dem man taken by di land, a bushman, y'know? Hidden because of dem skills. What dem call it? Camouflage? Me nuh know. Roun here di story of di Walker been use to frighten children for many years. No one ever see him. Some seh him a freeman, a obeah, or a myal man; others seh him a duppy of a freeman stalkin di lan, wreakin retribution on di evil doers, no matter where dem from. No one believe her. Even den di Walker was jus story. Me modder would run weh, belly out so, an try an find dat place in di jungle. She could not help herself, but she never find it.

Me poopa open her and let out what was left dere. We all have tings leff inna us dat should not be dere, tings left from a past dat not ours, tings dat grow dat we cyant tek out by weself. You hear me? All ah we. An if you meet di right man, di man dat fit you, dem let it out. Black woman carry di worl between we legs an pan we shoulder, carry it an carry it. Mus no mek man turn you fool. Dat is what me daughta do, like me modder, mek man turn she hidiat. Me? Man cyant do nuttin wid me. Dat is why me tek so much lick, but me don't care. A true me poopa was one ah di bush people. Him give she back to she self but it kill her. Some love like dat, y'know, can kill you. Me never love no man like dat. Man has one use. You hear me?

Me poor mama carry me fi a year, despite di beatings. When she time come, she have to be tied down to di bed. Big Pearl fear she go kill herself an dat was against God. What ever happen to she, she have to suffer di consequence. She was broken and silent. She seh she have no memory of di birth, but one day dere me was.

Likkle Pearl die when I still jus a baby, an she still a baby herself, but di one memory I have is of she screamin and sweepin an flashin her han all bout she head, like tryin to box invisible fly. She use fi weep all di time, an when she not weepin she shouting. It was after me born she start screamin. My modder could shout from sun-up to sundown and never miss a damn beat. Dat is why people say she crazy; dem could hear her across di valley, knowing she not talking to anyone in particular, she jus want mek noise. Now me tink she just making sure she not dead. As long as noise a come out, den she still here.

When me modder die, dem fine her many weeks later under a tree in a clearin no one ever seen before. Big Pearl seh dat dem have to chop di tree from around her. Some people seh as soon as di tree let she go she start shrivel up an stink up di place. Big Pearl Before Swine set fire to di tree an carry she chile back to di house. She chop off a big part of di cedar tree to mek Likkle Pearl a coffin, like dey doin fi me.

Marshall, in his office

Ever since I heard, I've felt – what? Troubled? Knew she was going, knew she was going to leave. Her eyes told me so, di same look as my fada had, as he lay in my arms and di light shut out.

... "What di backside you a do yah? Me know is you, is what you want?" She poked her stick through di shutters. "Me say, come out you mix-up, mix-up red devil!"

I came out, from behind di bush under her window, feeling foolish, like a boy. About a month ago. It was late. Don't know what possess me. It was three in di morning. I'd walked miles up to her window, in di duppy house. Dat night my whole body start to itch me, like me skin tryin to leave me bones an muscle behind. Couldn't sleep. My feet took me to her. I stood outside, watching, waiting, den suddenly me see her stick stabbin through di shutters and I heard her call me. She always knew when I was around. Even in di old days, she could tell I was near. When she open di shutters she see me an back away. She sat on di bed, her breathing heavy and quick.

"What you want wid me, red devil, what you want?"

"Want to see you."

"Well, you see me. Now move you dutty donkey-fucker self, before me scream."

"Look at you, Seduce, you lung can hardly hold di breath in you old body. What mek you tink you can scream. Even when you could, you never did."

"Yuh talk like a hidiat, always did. Anyway, look pan you! Yuh nearly ben over double, an dat likkle dutty, wrinkle-up piece a skin you have between you legs can't do nobody no harm any more."

"Did it harm you, Seduce?"

"Oh Christ pan di cross! Why don't you go an suck off di white man like you always do."

"Me! You suck off more white man dan me!"

"Yes, but dem haffi pay!"

"What is wrong wid you? I do me job, sumtin you people will never understand. I am di law."

"No you is not. Di white man across di sea is di law; you only work fi him."

"You work fi him too."

"No, no, no, me work fi meself."

"You still have di cutlass under you bed?"

"You want to come look fi it?"

Di old bitch did cut me, but not as bad as she want to, not as bad as she used to. She always hated me. She looked at me wid contempt, she always did, ever since di first time me see her.

I wear di face of me modder's rapist. I did not know her; she die when I born, but I always believe that my farder kill her. I also believe dat she was his daughter, but who knows? He was a drunkard. He'd worked on di plantations, an overseer, but he couldn't control di slaves when dey free. He always saw dem as slave. He loss his own place through lack of skill and no backbone. He did not have di heart for it. He become di man that count di cane, work out di tonnage, from place to place, countin and den drinkin. Di sugar man.

So me an me farder travel from plantation to plantation, looking fi work as temporary clerk. Him pass me off as his helper, but people see him in me. My eyes, my hands. People don't understand what it is to be poor and white on this island – another level of disrespect. Imagine being look down on by everybody. Di poorest blacks, dat live in di filth and muck of oddas, look at you an thank god dey not you. Every day I hated my life with my father. He drank what he could, spend di money on whores when his body let him. I watched him drown in his own filth. He told me tales of past wealth and position as if they would keep us alive.

"We're not meant to be here, my lad, oh no, we're from important people. Don't get comfortable, we don't belong here. Soon, my son, we'll go home and forget about this place an what it's done to us. They should never have sent me here. Blackguards! It was my brothers. I was the old man's favourite. Jealous brutes. I have written – and don't worry, I've told them all about you. You're my son. Son and heir. We'll be well set up back home. Ha! Just you wait. Where's the rum? Fetch it, you little black bastard! Or I'll leave you here with the other trash!" And so it went on. Then one day that old, dirty, useless man die in my arms. I can still smell his dying breath.

He left me in di care of an Indian woman who say she love him. But all she did was scrub my knees to bleeding, trying to get off di black. Then I went to war in Europe with the West India regiment.

Me never feel so cole. Is so cole, when you breathe out, there is nothing, not even no steam, no warm breath to tell you you livin. Only that space that hangs in di air where you breath should be. Di kind a cole dat di noise you hearin is you teeth, knockin in you head. And di strangest ting. Warm piss. Comin out you cole body. Is where dat piss get its heat from? I learn to do everyting wid my left hand cos di cole took my right. You ever hear pain? Di sound so deep and down from below ground that you don't know is who or what. It sounds like di earth cryin for itself. We weren't used to it, we had no idea such cole exist. The lieutenant wave us onto the ship, smiling, telling us bout king and country and serving a bigger purpose. We strolled on like we're going on holiday. When the waters turn icy, we're like black bugs crawling around, looking for any small places of heat and crowding round it. Men crying like babies for their modders. We begged di sea to rear up and take us. One fella called Flint – cos he easy to light – had too much flesh hangin off his small frame and women's hips, messin up his uniform. He threw himself overboard and let di cole take him to heaven, when di rest of us pray for the heat of hell.

Funny I should think of all this today. There was no funeral for my father, but there is one for dis whore who stop at nothing to get her own way.

In the bush outside the town square.

Loo

We forget why we here on dis rock – an den me rememba, an feel di little goose bumps raise on our skin. We was going to look for granddaddy. People say he was an everlivin bush man. Dat he took Likkle Pearl when she was nuttin but a chile, and what happen to her keep she a chile til she dead. People say dat she was gone fi weeks, an when people fine her, dem have to force she legs down and carry she back to di house, legs still high an it tek hot water an towels to get dem back down. Dat is what Nanny tell we. We want to know if granddaddy can help us. Odda people say is untrue, is not bushman but is duppy dat rape she.

But we cyant keep waitin here. Mus go back. Soon people will be lookin for us an dis part a di bush will be crawlin wid people. What's dat noise? No is nuttin. Everybody at Nanny funeral or di demonstration. We shouldn't feel fraid, for all di townspeople fraid of demselves, feel dat we mek dem scared, expose dem. Dat's what our brother Son use to say.

… "You know what is wrong wid you, Loo?"

We sittin with Son under di cedar in di front yard. We don't answer, for we have dis particular talk wid our brother fi long time. He soon going to di mainland; we only watch him chop firewood becas ourselves might not see him again. To be with him – not to talk. Our bredda hardly eva talk. But today, becas he want to tell me about meself, sudden him tongue loose like a Lampi.

"You know what is wrong wid you? You mek people feel naked, people feel naked when dem roun you."

"We do nuttin."

"You nuh have to do nuttin. You jus mek people uneasy."

"So uneasy, you runnin?"

"No, not runnin from you, runnin from here, from dis, from Nanny, an from… from Mama. From Lucretia. From all di tings dat holdin us down. Don't you want to be free?"

"We are free."

"No, no, you are not. You di most trap me see anyone trap."

"Trap, by wha?"

"By history, Loo, by history. Too many people, too many stories."

Dat is all he say. Him stop talking; dat is how him always stay. We see di look on him face dat says him done talk. Dat was years ago, an now him eyes still full but him mout empty.

Di poundin in we head soun like ole poco drums. We fill wid sorrow an… we feel stuck to di rock. Di pouch feel heavy on we side. Me hear di rustling of leaves. Who is dis, nuh? Honey Rock, he has found us.

"So, you got out unhurt?"

"Yes."

"Good, someone pulled me and I had to let go of you."

We sat and we see di sweat pour troo him fine clothes and collect on the ridges of him neck. A fine mainland man, well fed, red, a tiny moustache trim by someone else. He smack at his clothes, trying to free himself from di bush dust.

"My people warned me this has been happening everywhere. I only hope no one was seriously injured or worse."

He is turning, looking for a way out.

"Do you care?"

He swings back to me. "Of course I care. We're in this together. If Black men cannot see each other as one, we'll perish."

He is panting. Di heat and hotness is forcing out his breath, so I can see his chest, rise and fall under di wet shirt. He is looking at we, looking at him.

"What's your name?"

"We have many."

"What is your name today?"

"Loo."

He bows low and takes my hand. "It's a pleasure to meet you, Loo, and my name is..."

"We know your name."

He looks confuse but not worried. As if it is di most natural thing in the worl for we to hear of him.

"How do we get out of here?"

"We have no wish to leave."

"I need to catch my boat. Which direction is the harbour?"

"They will be looking for you."

He winks a black eye and the lids go across like a snake and he says, "I know."

He catches our tongue in him mout and leads us to a tree. He holds ourselves with his breath, like the strongest rope, and we can do nothing but follow. He puts our legs around him and keeps our tongue. We have no need for it. His hands all over our neck and back, he dig his fingers into our rump as he holds us against the tree and whispers, "It is time for us to go back home." The tree bark is rough and it pierce the shirt he's lifting so he can put we breas' in his mouth and talk of freedom, of the Black man's struggle and the white man's hatred. He presses his fingers through our drawers and rubs our penny til it is wet like early mornin rain an shinin new, and talks about labour and the working man. He sucks at our lips like a new born and mutters about di loss of history. As he pull we down, to lie between di tree roots, and push our legs up and wide as far as dey can go, he sing dat every goddess needs her god. He mines our body, looking for di way in and di way out, still speaking of the role of the Black man. His city sweat fall in our eyes, burnin. When he rolls off weself, he smiles to the sky and talks about economic stability, sighs about the struggle and the leaders that are needed. When he fixes himself back into his trousers, he mumbles bout liberty. We will not see him again.

Will Nanny forgive us. We know she is free. Will she tink it spite? Will she be wid Big Mama Pearl Before Swine and

Likkle Pearl? Will Lucretia gather dem all up to her? No, we know she is waitin fi ourselves.

Di Lampis are comin. Dey go search for Nanny. Di poco drums are comin. Our soul knocks at our ribcage, beats behind our eyes. She is coming…

Seduce's house

Seduce

Me love a man wid a slow, slow smile. Di smile haffi tek time, dance roun him head, play wid him eyes an mout and finally creep to him lips. A slow smile always get me. Glory farder, Washington, had a slow smile, an di rest of him not dat quick eider. You see me? Me love a man wid a tight-up batty. Batty haffi be high an shine. Loose batty no good. Like di batty me rememberin now, skin foldin into legs, join by creases dat look like a map to nowhere. Small flowers of renkin stench spring from all about him body.

..."You no hear slavery done?"

"Don't talk to me like that, I will not have you talking to me like that."

"Me seh, slavery done."

"Oh don't, don't madam..."

"You want a floggin?"

"No, no."

"Me seh you want a floggin?"

"By God, I do not."

"Me tink you do. You want me to strip off di flesh from you bones?"

"No, madam, I most certainly do not, I most, most certainly..."

I uncurled di whip an lash him, two, three, four times. Flesh not broken but red up an swell. When di pain lick him, him change him tone.

"Black bitch, abominable damnation, heathen, heathen, devil..."

Dem always cry devil when dem ah look pan we. Always a cry devil.

"Unholy thing, sent to torment my soul."

"You mek too much noise, Farder, too much noise."

"No more, madam; it is enough."

I yanked pan di leather strap bindin him to the post in the corner of di shack. I borrow Maybell's for this. I did not want this man inna me home. All di Lampis surprise when I turn up dat mornin. I hadn't been back to Paradise for many years, ten or more. When dem learn what me was dere to do, dem offa me Maybell place. She was ol, older dan me an tired. She was dere when me start but me nuh know how ole she was by den. Di Lampis was trying to look afta her an she need di money. Lampi life tek its toll on her, an she have but di one eye. People seh di odda one jump out her head when it did see all di tings it have to see. Sometime pickney mek up dat dey see Maybell eye hiding inna tree, near she shack. Too fraid to go back to her.

I sat at a small table, eating an orange. Dere is nuttin betta dan a sweet orange, an mine is di bes pan di island. I eat slow, let him wait, you cyant rush a good orange. So me jus sit an eat – him in di corner, cryin, chattin, pleadin, cursin me, him pink skin glowin red. I could hear Maybell an some a di Lampis outside a laugh. We all like to hear di reverend cry out an beg.

"You soun so piggish; is you a pig, reverend?"

"I might be a pig, but if I wanted to marry your ugly black hide, you would not say no."

"You tink so?"

"I know it. Within you is the devil, within me is salvation and don't think I do not know who you are. You come from a long line of murderers and thieves."

"Is true. Yuh want me commit murder now?"

"Let me go, madam, we will have no more of this."

"What you talkin?"

"I said let me go."

"Let us pray, reverend..."

"Blasphemer."

"Let us pray dat me han get tired. What is wrong wid you people? Don't you know you time nearly done?"

"Shut up, shut up. If you mean that pathetic little event when you killed those godfearing people – that was years ago and look, we are still here."

"Yes, wid you backside out waitin for me whip."

"It is your time that is nearly done."

He was right. Was not only Maybell sufferin. People across di water stop wantin di lampi so much again. Di Lampi life was goin, I could see dat, even from di top of me hill.

I get up slow an beat him, beat him.

"Black whore, nigger whore. I will see you hanged for this."

When him talk, me beat more, di new welts joinin di old ones.

"You nigger bitch of Satan, I'll see you fry in hell, you'll be damned, you an your kind, sons and daughters of Ham, I'll see you dead, bitch, dog, heathen, heathen!"

He paid me an left. Me? I was tired, me ches feel tight an sweat had broke out ova me wid di effort, but dese white people strange an strange an stranger still. Me give Maybell her piece an walk it up di hill to me house. As me get nearer, me see Glory sitting pan di porch, Son nex to her, an Loo was dancing for dem in the yard. Bag pack, Son ready to leave di home I had worked hard for. He was goin to di mainland for his education. One a dem church school di pickney dem live in. When I got to dem I held out di money, still damp wid me sweat. She take it, neva ask where it come from, an den she left to tek Son to di dock.

Outside Seduce's house

The Lampis

"Let the white lilies fall."

"Let dem ease you spirit."

"Catch di scent of dem in the air."

"Wash in lily water, ease you mine."

"Wash in lily water, ease you spirit."

"Let dem fall so that you can walk."

"Walk"

"But look eeee? Every man from here to di mainlan and back is in attendance."

"Me hear seh Son ah just come."

"What you ah seh?"

"It is only right an fittin, grandpickney no mus come?"

"Me nah see dat bwoy in maybe ten years or more."

"Him always strange, have di look ah him poopa."

"Untamed spirit."

"Be quiet, see him yah!"

"He's here!"

Son

All these people, all these woman. The prodigal returned! Can't wait for this to be over, get back to normality. So tired. My addiction's come back. God, how I need one, but have to wait. Until these women go away, until I'm on my own. The sad fate of being a working Black man – brings out all the desperate Black women. They're all looking at me, expecting something, wanting so very much for me to do something, but as always, when I reach here, I can't do a thing. Just being here stops me. My palms are sweating. Where's my hankerchief? One of the white ones that Mama sends every year. Does she think we don't have them over there? Still, I do use them. I'm so tired of being looked at. A dog in the circus? What trick should I perform? They wouldn't like my only real talent. How shocked the good ladies would be. God, it's all so disgusting. Mama hopes that one day I'll return, but I've lived more there than here, and the weight of her longing turns my mouth sour. I'll have to choose my moment to tell Ma I'm not staying.

I'd just dismissed the class, packing up the books. It felt as though someone was pushing a hot needle through my heart. Small, small, concentrated pain that took away my breath and the strength in my legs. I had to sit down fast and when I'd recovered, knew there was no choice: I had to come back. Don't know what you call it – Nanny, Mama, Loo, Lucretia, me? – don't know and don't care. Except for Loo, it's all the same. Head's throbbing – a pump in my ears that beats out of time with my heart. Sometimes it blocks out every other sound, so loud I'm sure every one else can hear it. Used to ask people, "Can you hear that?" They'd look at me, puzzled. But when I do what I do, it goes away. Stumbled on the solution by chance, desperate to feel normal. Came to me in a wash of connection to my body and what it needed, almost separate from myself. When I do it, everything is right again. The noise, the sweating, my running shadow can rest a moment. Then I'm happy, bright, almost carefree. The truth of all addictions. You're another person when you've answered that unending call. You can cope, see, feel and hear again.

Nanny wanted me to go into the church. Call it her revenge. One of her own, under the gaze of God, but I couldn't stand it. Watch myself too hard for anyone else to watch me. The restrictions on your behaviour, the constant acknowledgement of sin, that just living and breathing creates sin – we're all better off dead. At least in death we're in God's house. Rubbish! Pastor Collins and I had the talks, but I chose teaching…

…"You're no use to me, no God use!" She was screaming.

I was standing at the foot of the bed, the last time I was here. Mama stood by the door, wanting to cover me from the loudness of the hatred spewing out of Nanny's mouth.

"No use, no use. Get out, get out! Ah you do him so."

She picked up some slippers by the bed and threw them weakly at Mama. Mama ran; they would never have reached her, but old habits die hard.

"Move fram me wid you raw eye, move!"

I didn't but I kept my raw eye on her. I enjoyed it. The rattle from her chest rose high in the room, searching for corners to hide in.

"Galang, move!"

I didn't. As she lay back down I wondered who or what she saw.

"You want fi torment me?"

"No, Nanny."

"You wan fi kill me?"

"No, Nanny."

"Den wah?"

"I am not going to apologise, I'm not going to say sorry. I do not want to be a priest, a pastor, monk or any type of churchman. I'm not a hypocrite. With their nasty ways, getting fat while their congregations grow hungry, drinking rum and preaching sobriety. All those parents hoping to buy a place in heaven with their children. I've seen it too often. We give those devil-workers too much power."

"Talk hinglish, talk like weh you come fram. You houghty-toughty ways not to use pon you own people."

"Ah you sen me deh."

"Fi you heducation, fi di bettament of di family, so you..."

"What bout what me want?"

"It not never bout you!"

"The church rotten to the core, it invent by white people to keep us enslaved. Dey don't even believe it as much as we do. My God, Nanny, I know you don't believe."

"What I believe and know is two different ting. Anyway what me believe ent matter."

"Where's the shrine you had under di house bottom here, Nanny? Who you praying to? You don't figet yuh old ways."

She seemed to be fighting with the covers. She clawed at them and wisps of white hair left her head and flew out of the window.

"Dat is why you have to be a churchman, you nuh see it? So dat you can change tings."

No, I didn't see it, but I saw she didn't really want me to change anything. She wanted me to corrupt it. The noise in my head grew. I could feel every one of my teeth in my head. My eyes needed to shut.

"Get out, wutless, nasty bwoy. Go do wah you a go do. Go fix you demon. You ah go bline, maybe den we can all res easy an you can be reasonable."

She turned towards the window. The shock and shame opened my mouth. She knew. How could she? Wily old woman, she knew more than she ever told us. Humiliation crept along my body, like heat rash, the bumps filling with water. I wanted to be thought well of. Should I explain, try to reason?

"Nanny… I…"

"Yuh have more in common wid di church dan you wan to admit. You have a lot to tank church fah."

"Nanny…"

"Get out!"

That was the last time I was here, seven years ago. And here I am, the noise of clacking female tongues clinging to my black funeral clothes, the noise of Mama's loss and release and the noises of Loo, lost and desperate to be found. How does Collins do it? Now he wants me to speak. I just got here…

Marshall's office

Marshall and Loo

"Enter."

The young clerk stepped into the room. First with purpose, then faltering as he came closer. Until he was almost falling over by the time he reached him. Marshall didn't look up, but kept reading a report about some young man who wanted to go back to Africa and take his so-called people with him. The report had the colourful emblem of authority at the top and the governor's signature at the bottom. He rubbed his thumb along the signature. It smudged slightly. He felt irritable. Arrests had been made but the agitator had escaped. He was staring at his thumb when the boy came in and fell towards him. He continued to stare at it. The clerk wondered what was wrong with his thumb.

"Shall I get a dressing, sir?"

"What?"

"Shall I..."

"What is it?"

His room was lined with the pictures of past governors. All white or pretending to be. The whole room was white and he its only shadow.

"Well?"

"There's someone to see you, sir."

They both waited for each to speak.

"Do you want me to guess, private?"

"No, no, sir. It's that girl sir, that mad gyal, Loo. She says she's not leaving until she sees you."

He didn't want to see her and was embarrassed by her audacity. How dare she presume it was alright to come here? His place of work. His place. Like they were friends or colleagues.

"Send her in." He should tell her about her backside.

She slipped into the room on silent, bare feet, the scarf on her head tilted sideways. She had her grandmother's eyes.

"What do you want?" He wanted to be stern, he wanted to make her afraid and ashamed. They had nothing in common and he knew by now that the whole barracks would know she was there to see him.

She breathed quietly, a small leather pouch swinging from her waist. He presumed it was some superstitious sumting. He tried to outstare her, but he couldn't and found his eyes resting on that small leather pouch.

"You know I can have you placed under arrest?"

"Yes."

She did not move and he started to feel outnumbered, outgunned. He smashed his hand on the table, to shake her and himself.

"What d'you you want?"

"We want you to arrest us."

"For that fool fool demonstration? What do you know about it?"

He already knew the answers.

"Do you know the leader?"

For the first time she cast her eyes down.

"Not much."

He stood and turned to the window, so she could not see his face.

"What is it? I got no time for foolishness today. If you want to go to the jailhouse, to earn some money like your grandmother use to, then you're out of luck. We don't allow that kind of thing any more."

"If yuh tryin to hurt us, you won't get satisfaction."

"What?"

"We want to be arrested, we want to be taken in. We've committed a crime."

Outside, the noises of the town played. People laughing, swearing, screaming, dying. The girl was strange, always was. And yet not a girl. A woman. Wild, loose, wandering around with no supervision, no shoes. She lived in a world of her own, of we instead of I. Did it make her dangerous? He'd caught her, one evening, kneeling by the fork in the road just outside town. She didn't see him and he didn't want to give her anything to talk to him about, so he moved by as quickly as he could. He looked at her hard. She would always be a girl, never a woman. She had that about her. Maybe that's why the island men left her alone, not because of some legend, or because they were scared of her, but because she looked like all their daughters. There was never any scandal about her. No women came to him to complain that she had taken their man. No one said she stole anything or even so much as spit on the ground. But she wasn't really a girl and soon, not so long now, her face would show it.

"Well?"

"Take us away."

"What have you done?"

Her hand fluttered to the pouch and then back down by her side.

"What's in there?"

"Our stories."

"What is this?"

She reached into the pouch and pulled out a handful of what looked liked herbs and bits of dry leaf and scattered them on the table in front of them. He recoiled, stood up sharply and knocked the chair over behind him.

"What you tryin to do?" He lunged for her and she fell backwards. He stood over her and hit her head, dragged off her scarf, tried to punch and kick her.

"What d'you think you're doing?"

"We..."

"What the hell is it?"

"Herbs"

"What are they for?"

"Blessed death, longed for sleep."

His blows were feeble and he made the noises of a once

strong man who now resorted to slapping and pushing instead of punching. He couldn't remember the last time his hand had made a fist. She took the soft beating. Even though she had the strength to crush this little, angry man, she didn't want to. And he knew it. Which made him more angry, his weakness displayed. She sighed, as if every blow released her.

"You're not going to arrest we?"

"Get up!"

"But…"

"Go back to you mad family, mad bitch. I'm not wasting any more time on you today."

"We…"

"Get out!"

She hesitated a moment, unsure, unsteady.

"We..."

"Go!"

He watched the door close and at the same time closed his eyes. He felt the side of his head throbbing. Maybe he should go. There was bound to be trouble. But he had to use everything within him to keep himself contained.

FOURTH MOVEMENT

Seduce's house

The world collapsed and stiffened. Seduce stared into space and counted the tiny specks of dust collecting around her guests. She was goin to meet the earth that spawned her, the sky that belched her, the sea that contained her thousand deaths, and in it she would find her face.

"Bwoy, time short eeee?"

Feet stamped in the dirt, puffs of red earth flew around them, beating out the time of heartbeats.

Seduce looked on. She was unaffected by what was happening. She was impatient to leave, bored.

Watch dem. What ah set ah jackarse. Don't dey see dat life nothing more dan dat – life, and now everyting mess up and we haffi grab it back. Grab it all back.

"Grab it back. Grab it all back," the Lampis said together.

Outside the house, the Lampis sat around the cooking pot, talking, finalising. Inside, the guests were milling about, eating slowly and feeling quickly. The coffin was in the middle of the parlour. Guests peered in. Son was in a corner, nodding as people smiled at him, but no one talked to him, except Mikey, and he was tired of avoiding the old man. He stared at his plate, wondered where Loo was. Maybe she should come back with him to the mainland where he could take care of her. He fought the desire to run out to be by himself. Glory was in the kitchen, sitting at the table, women leaning into her, creating a wall to keep gossip in, but her story would leak out. It was in the body of her daughter. Pastor Collins stood by the coffin, his hand gently sitting on its wooden edge. He tried to ignore his leg, which wanted to climb in with Seduce. He didn't understand why somehow the breath travelling around his body didn't seem to be his. He panted quietly. He didn't want his wife or mother to see, or even be a part of what he was feeling. He needed to do this on his own. Mikey sat in a chair on the porch, near the Lampis. He always enjoyed their company. He didn't understand the people inside. Glory's church women. They reminded him too much of his mother and he didn't want to think about her today. He wanted his mind to rest on Seduce, wanted her to come to him, to be with him and remember him.

The stillness in the air held them. Forced their hands quiet, held down tongues, stopped hair from moving and kept skirts captive. Sweat encased them and bound them together. Something was going to happen. Glory knew what some of them wanted, what they had been waiting for. The noise and laughter of the Lampis had taken her nerves to a nakedness she had never felt before.

Hyacinth stayed close to Glory, as always happy to be in the middle of someone else's business. Her mouth ran water with anticipation. Alfredo tried his best to lose his wife, but somehow she found him, eased herself onto him, put her arm round his waist, a hand on his shoulder. He felt uncomfortable; he knew what she was doing and so would every one else as well. But Seduce was gone. What had anybody to fear?

"You have fed us so well..." Hyacinth tried to keep Glory's attention. She didn't know why, only that she had to play a part.

No one knew where the drummers had come from. They stood in a row, decided by the size of the drums. They beat them with sticks until it seemed the world moved to their beat, pounding, talking, shaking, pushing hearts further towards the ground, making pelvises draw nearer to the earth. One by one the people started to hear their story.

"My god, she's here!"

"Di mad gyal come back."

"She look bad, eee?"

Everyone turned to see Loo come in. She looked dirty and beaten. Glory rushed over to her.

"Where have you been?"

"We... can't remember."

"Go and wash up. Hurry!"

"No."

"I said..."

"How nice, my dear, dat everyone is here. I suppose dat is di only good ting bout funerals." Hyacinth's voice rode high, allowing every one to catch it.

Loo stood in a corner, by the coffin. Herselves felt no shame, only remorse. They wished that time wasn't in such a hurry. Pastor Collins stood and stared through the window, disgusted, mesmerised by the Lampis and the drummers, thinking how the air can smell death as well as life, because it shares the space with both.

Son felt only contempt for the women trying to comfort Glory, surrounding his mother with false kindness and church righteousness. He didn't want to feel anything today, least of all for her. She soaked in the sympathy, sucked long and hard at the mournful words, sad whispers about loss and life carrying on, she goes to a better place, she's in the house of Her father. Ha! Seduce gave thanks for not knowing her father. Would that be another man wanting something from her? Glory accepted the touches on her shoulders, back and arms from women who had previously damned her. This was her time.

Son continued to stare at his plate. The food changed shape in front of him. He hadn't eaten like this in a long time. He wondered what it would be like to sit always in this wilderness, to think that all this colour, shine, life, movement was yours. He felt jealous of Loo, but he had never belonged here.

"We have come!" The Lampis stood by the door, knives and cutlasses out. The guests did not stir, did not look up, as if by avoiding their eyes they would be able to avoid their anger and knowledge. No one had seen them come in; they were just there.

"Give us what is ours."

Glory's mouth moved in horror. No sound came out but

she ran over to the coffin, with arms outstretched, mirroring her beloved Christ, trying to protect Seduce from damnation.

"Tek her if you tink you bad."

"It is her time now. Time for her to go."

"We tek she home."

"She's not going nowhere. What in Jesus' name is wrong wid you? She haffi go inna di ground. It's what she…"

"No, don't seh dat."

"It's not what she want."

"You know what she want?"

"Get out!"

"Yuh know, betta dan anyone, dat di dead talk."

"I said get out."

"Don' try to stop us."

"How dare you! You were not invited."

"We were."

"Not by me!"

"No, not by you. She called us here." They pointed to the coffin, and to Loo.

"Tek her den, do what you want. I've washed my hands of it."

Glory made her hands wash the air; the air fought her, her movements were slow. But she did not move. She screamed inside. She could fall, throw herself over the coffin, lash out, beat them, but she knew she couldn't win. So she turned, with shame and desperation pouring out of her, to the only person she thought could help.

"If you ever wanted to do sumting for her, do it now." Spit and ashes came to mind and she felt the taste in her mouth and she wanted to throw up. "Come on, boy!"

"I am no longer a boy."

"I don't care what your name is. Don't you see? We have to do this under God, or we will all be blasphemers. Help Mama."

Pastor Collins didn't speak. He could only use his mouth to taste his own tears.

Hyacinth felt that as he was her son, by proxy and as such, she had the right to speak for him.

"You Lampis, get out!"

"No!"

"We cyant do it."

"She has to go home."

"Let her go."

Glory didn't move and the Lampis took a step towards her.

"As you wish it."

"No!"

"Someone get Marshall."

"He's here."

Everyone watched him climb out of the big, black, government car, slowly, painfully. He pushed his way through the crowd and through the Lampis to stand next to Glory.

"What is going on here?"

"Oh thank God, praise him. Marshall, they have come for Mama. Mek dem stop."

He looked at the Lampis, he looked at the crowd. The machetes and cutlasses whistled as the wind passed over them. He couldn't bear to look behind him, at the husk of the woman he had hated and loved for as long as he could remember. His hands shook.

"Move back!"

But his voice faltered and he let the Lampis pass him and go over to the coffin. Something in Glory burst out like a dam breaking.

She screamed, "Whores! Yes, go on, kill me, like you kill other people. Yuh Lampis love no one but yuhself. Yuh behaviour lawless, yuh ways is pagan, you don't love her, you don't know anyting about her. I've had to do every God ting! Even when she took my children love from me!"

"It was you that didn't love us!" Son couldn't stand how his mother's voice was making him feel.

"She gave me no choice. And what are you doin here now? For me or she? Becas she call you? She neva cared about you!"

"Yes she did, she saved me."

"Oh shut up, fool! Sick fool! All of you fools! Where were you when she cry, when she couldn't feed herself, when she watch she body bloat and shrink and her hair fall out? Where..."

Dat gyal gon too damn clear! Seduce felt offended to hear

her daughter display her illness in front of everyone. She blocked it out, found herself on the roof and liked it there. She could see everything.

"Is dis what you want, for it to be like dis? Yuh Godless!"

"Why Mama, dis have nuttin to do wid us. Is what happening. Nanny would've..." Loo had never spoken to her mother like this before. She had never seen herself as her equal.

"What you know bout Nanny? What you know bout dat woman?"

"We know nuff..."

"We! We? There is no we. You mad! Chupid, fool fool gyal! You listen to her blasphemous stories, her lies of murder and ancestors dat never was and it turn yuh mind. You fool fool gyal; she was a dutty, stinkin' ole whore!"

Loo stepped across the room and slapped her mother hard across her face. She stared at her hand as if she had no control over it and ran out. She stood waiting for the others.

The skin on Hyacinth's body was hot all over. This was more than she ever thought could happen. What now?

"Enough!"

"We here."

"We've never gone away."

"Watchin and waitin..."

"For what? Do you think you mek sense? You cannot tek her way from she family."

"We are her family."

"Marshall! Do sumting!" Hyacinth shouted. She pushed through the crowd. "Get out blasphemers!"

"Mind you tongue, les we tek it wid us."

"Whores of Satan!"

Seduce licked her lips. Maybe someone would give Hyacinth the backsiding she deserved. Dat is worth dyin fah!

Hyacinth turned to her son who was hypnotized by his own grief, and suddenly she knew he would never feel this way for her.

"Come son," she urged him. She clung to his arm and tried to get him to look down at her.

"Teach dem, my boy, show dem di way." She clutched his hand to her chest and waited for him to respond, but he wasn't looking at her. He was looking towards the coffin.

"Lissen me, lissen me, you have to show dem di way; you're the only man of God here, you… you…"

The words fell stone cold out of her mouth and onto the floor.

Hyacinth thought of all the years of taking in other people's washing. Of cooking other people's food. Of tending to other people's needs so that sometimes she didn't know where she stopped and they began. Of working in that linen shop in town, looked down upon by the middle-class browns who saw her black face as a reminder of who they didn't want to be. She took it all to send her boy to school. To get him away from here. When her nails cracked, she smiled; when her body ached, she prayed. She was doing God's work by creating a man of God. He would be grateful to her forever.

"Mama, I… I can't."

He looked down at her crushed, weak body and felt ashamed of himself. She wanted so much and he could give her so little. She took a step back and looked him up and down, as if this was the first time she had seen him.

"I shoulda lef you inna di rass clart bush!"

People stared at her. Spit and hatred steamed out of her mouth. How dare he take this away from her.

"I prayed dis day would never come."

"I…"

"Jesus pan di cross, what does it take? What does it take for you to see, with yuh own damn eyes? You fool, you chupid useless fool!"

"Don't!"

"You shame me! You shame me!"

"What?"

"That yuh true blood would show out itself, now at dis time. That you woulda mek me shame. I tried to mek you godly, but dere ain't nuttin to be done wid a soul already damned!"

"Mama, please."

"I am not your modder; she is!"

Hyacinth ran to the coffin to try and topple it over, but Pastor Collins fought her, held her hands that wanted to claw at him and Seduce. He pushed her away and she fell into the crowd. People tried to help her to stand and restrain her at the same time.

"I found you! You would be dead, if not for me! She left you dere to kill you! So di bush would claim you, but I saved you!"

Pastor Collins' wife, who had fought for her place in his heart, ran out crying. Her husband had abandoned himself.

Geno? Could it be? Mikey stared up at him and the wonder of life and parenthood seeped into his bones. "Geno?" he whispered. He wanted his mouth to get used to it.

Shock crept around the people. Pastor Collins let go of the woman he had never felt connected to. Seduce was his mother. Some had always suspected it. The old ones, who remembered the baby, thought they could see it now.

Why had no one noticed before?

The good ladies gathered their things, men looked for discarded hats. Alfredo stepped up and put a hand on Collins' arm. Words were useless. His wife tugged at him.

"It's time to go." They all started to leave. And Glory watched her hard-won respectability crumble.

"Please, please. We haven't finished"

Seduce blew a breeze to dry the tears on her son's face. Me know. And all the love she could wrench from her muscles and sinews and marrow, the deep dark point in her that she'd carried and wanted so much to give, she let it go. It flew around the room and settled on his shoulders.

Mikey felt that his blood had betrayed him, his bones had let him down, his muscles had worked against him, had served to keep him blind. The times he'd chased that boy from under the house, the times he'd hit him around the head when the boy had annoyed him for hanging around. And here he was. Mikey shook his head, heavy with his hair wound around it like a halo. He'd always distrusted Collins as a preacher. He believed that the fruit never fell too far from the tree, blood was thicker than water, like father like son. But he'd never felt this about him. He was Pastor Collins. He didn't know him, had never known him, had only been willing to talk to the boy because Seduce asked him to. Then he felt his pains recede. He wasn't alone any more. He had a son. But what hurt him was why he hadn't recognized him. The time lost. The last time he'd known him as his son, the child was just a few months old, with his mother's eyes and his father's wandering spirit.

"If you put im dung, as Jah beholds, im garn. Me tell you seh di pickney cyant walk, cyant talk, not even crawl, yet Jah know, dat child move from place to place."

So when Seduce calmly walked up to his boat and said, "Where di bwoy?" he wasn't worried. He knew they would find him but they never did and it broke his body and his heart. And now, the betrayal of his own blood, not to recognize itself, how could it do this to him? How could she? She must've known. And a red pressure formed in his chest that he struggled to breathe out. He had felt sure, sure that if his eyes ever again saw his boy, they would tell him. He would know. He was disgusted with himself. The body that for so long had carried him, that for so long had claimed his sympathy, had begged him to root himself to it, had begged for attention from a woman consumed with herself, now, now, now, it was truly broken. The stick he carried, made shiny by his sweat and skin, began to shake, because he was shaking. He lifted the stick and swung it round his head before it fell on Hyacinth with a crack that sounded like unseen small shells being broken by deliberate feet. Seduce danced. No one made a sound. Hyacinth dropped.

"She dead?" A crowd gathered round her; a prayer was heard from somewhere.

"Me don' know why me do it. God speak and tell me to tek him to save him, I..."

Marshall stared ahead of him. Waiting for this to be over. He had always prided himself on his self-control. Embarrassed, he feared to lose it now. When Glory tried to throw herself at the Lampis, he grabbed her, shouting, "Do you want to join your mother?"

Son

The Lampis claimed her. My mother shouted and spat her particular form of love and rejection. Pastor Collins seemed rooted to the spot. He'd lost his voice and strength as his wife and mother yelled around him. My uncle! I couldn't hope for better! The only other man in my family, a useless, gibbering idiot! Loo stands quietly, waiting for the Lampis while the town's people, the good men and women of Church, watch on, filled with a kind of terror, not knowing what to do.

The Lampis followed the drummers and we followed them.

"Mama."

"Where are you going?"

"Mama." Loo was trying to coax my mother. "Mama, come."

Mama's water-filled eyes looked at the people around her and she decided not to disappoint.

"Go, go! Godless bitches, into the arms of Satan!"

Loo went to Collins.

"Come, Uncle." He nodded silently.

She walked away, then stopped and looked at me.

"We honour our dead, we honour our ancestors, we honour our family, we do what we need to. Help us."

I was taken aback. How could I help? I wasn't even sure I wanted to. But I trusted Loo so I followed. Loo seemed to need me, the only woman that ever did. When I got outside, I couldn't see which direction she had taken, but I already knew.

Marshall and Glory

Marshall sat at the table in the kitchen. Glory stood by the open door, watching them disappear into the bush. Hyacinth was still outside, crying and praying in the dirt that her son had left her in. Her high, desperate voice travelled inside the kitchen and irritated them. Marshall looked at Glory. He did not want to comfort her, did not want to stay, but her sorrow drew him to her in a way that made him think about himself. They could hear the drums in the distance, like mosquitoes ready to help themselves to their blood.

Glory moved about the room as if it was new and she didn't quite know where she was, as if she had lost something, but hadn't noticed that people had left or that Seduce had begun her journey home.

"Sit down, m'dear. It's over."

She sat down and she didn't know why. She stood up and sat down again. He looked at her vagueness and felt sorry for her. He had no wish to touch her or make her feel better, but he did touch her, as one would touch a child, an ignorant, unschooled child.

"You can't reach these people."

"Is what you seh?"

"You can't teach them. You lose, Glory. Dey will never be any more or less than what they are."

"What have I done?"

"You have been true to yourself. Did you want to go with them?"

"No." She looked at Marshall as if seeing him for the first time. He wore his age around his eyes and jaw. His jowls hung down and made him look as if he'd eaten something sour.

"Are you me father?"

He laughed uncomfortably. "No child, I am not. But, I will tell you, there were many who could've been."

"Why is this happening?"

"I told you, they are lost."

"Well, I won't be lost. I will not give up my soul for her, I will not! That at least is mine to do what I want with it."

"If you believe in such things."

"You don't?"

"I believe in what I can see. From where I stand, you can swap one magic for another."

"Then why did you let them go?"

He didn't want to answer that one. He rubbed his hands together, the cold never left them. He did not want his status to change from authority to man.

"To prevent bloodshed. I told you, it's as though them jus come off the boat. You'll learn."

"Are you a coward?"

"No, I'm a realist and you…"

"Me…?"

"You're a romantic, something your mother never was."

He picked up his hat with a flourish. All this had taken too much of his time already.

"They'll all be sorry." It was the one thing that Glory truly hoped for.

Anger was where Glory lived. It poured out of her skin, settled around her mouth, was like a suit of clothes without which she would be naked. She looked at her reflection and saw what she didn't have, what she thought the world and her mother owed her. She had long surrounded herself with herself. Before she did anything, committed herself to any action, she asked how was this different to what her mother would do, how did she and God feel about it? Was it the right thing to do?

She stared not at Collins but just above him. He had to resist the urge to look up. There he was, the baby she had known and the boy she had hated. What would God think of her now? She was always willing to… to… She started praying and her bottom lip trembled like someone who knew they were going to hell. But Geno had been the needlesharp point of fine glass that punctured her heart and created the hole where her mother's love had rushed out of her and towards him. Surely that wasn't right. And when he was lost, deep inside the bush, in between the mango roots where she had placed him, she thought no one would find him and then and then Seduce would look at her as she looked at him.

"Hey!" She stood up and called out. "Hey, where are you? Is where you gone?" Her voice echoed empty and became the voice of a searching child but nothing answered.

Pastor Collins drew up his six-foot body, uncurled it, breathed strength into his arms and legs and strode out behind the house. He saw Mikey ahead. He followed the sound of the drums.

FIFTH MOVEMENT

Outside Seduce's house, on the way up the hill.

Pastor Collins and Mikey.

"I and I could never tink, could not have hoped... Well, well, it's here."

"What's here?"

"Di day, di day, son, di day."

"What day?"

"Di day I and I fine you, we fine each other."

"You're not making sense, Uncle."

"I'm not you uncle."

"I know."

"What? You disappoint?"

"I don't know."

They walked on the soft grass, following the drums as they went deeper into the bush.

"Is what you ah do here?"

"I beg your pardon?"

"Don't beg me nuttin and answer di question."

"I..."

"You don't know, is it? Family, Jah know, family..."

The breeze pulled at their clothes. Mikey's hand trembled as he leaned heavily on his staff.

"Wait, mek we res."

Pastor Collins didn't want to rest, didn't want to do anything that anyone told him to do ever again.

"Help me, nuh!"

Pastor Collins took Mikey by the elbow and led him to sit under a silk cotton tree.

"The body betrays. As wid all tings, you mus know dat."

Pastor Collins stood awkwardly over the old man. Mikey looked up at the belly above him. He took his staff and gently tapped it.

"Too much white flour."

Pastor Collins cleared his throat, tried to pull in his belly, adjusted his trousers.

"Give me you han."

Pastor Collins did, wondering what the old man was going to do. Mikey took a small twig and drew something on his palm.

"You know dis?"

"No."

"Come, feel it again."

"What do you want from me?"

"I and I have no need of anyting. I and I want to give."

"What is it?"

"Something me shoulda give you long time. One ting I regret: your God isn't mine. You've been taught by your false modder dat Jah is hate and fear. No man should fear him farder so. Respec him, yes, but di trembling fear, me no hold nuttin to it. Jah is love, son. What we doin here right now, Jah present."

He took out his pipe and lit it. He watched the smoke curl up into the tree. His spirit smoothed out.

"Come, tek in some inspiration... Slowly, you lungs won't know what it is."

Pastor Collins stared at the pipe. My God, what is happening to me? Who have I become? But even though he knew that he would regret it, he sucked in the sweet, bitter smoke and held his breath. It felt like his throat was on fire. He choked and coughed; water came to his eyes.

"Again."

He didn't want to but everything was different now and maybe he needed to be different too. He felt that he had been asleep, but the clearest, shiniest sleep he'd ever had. He stretched out his hands and his fingers wrapped themselves around everybody he loved, had ever loved. He longed to hold his children. The colours touched him, even in the darkness; the wind settled his nerves; the heat from the day rose up to meet him. He was on the ground, sitting next to his father.

The drums were fading.

"Quick, we mus catch up."

He helped Mikey to his feet. He was smiling and nodding. The brightness of the night excited him. He felt all things possible. He walked along, next to the man he'd held as a baby, fifty years ago. Things come. Things truly come.

"How?"

"Huh?" Mikey was lost in his world, amazed by it. Jah was good.

"How did it happen?"

"Yuh no hear you false modder? You were so small, but a few months. She fine you, run to her people in di country, couple years and then come back. How was we to know?"

"She knew."

Pastor Collins used his head to point in the direction of the drums.

"No."

"Yes, how could she not?"

"Well maybe. But she have she reasons. What a fine upstanding man you turn out to be."

"Upstanding? You mean respectable?"

"Of course."

"Respectable and unhappy. That's not a successful life is it?"

"Well…"

"No! I'm sad and ridiculous, with women in my life that want more than any human should be asked to give."

"Ha ha. We is man, we all inna dat position."

They both laughed.

Before Hyacinth had sent him away, Mikey felt that the boy was a pest. He still had a hole in his body that ached and this boy had reminded him of it. He was always hiding bout the place, in the yard, under the house. Mikey had chased him away many times, thinking he was one of dem boys, hanging round, trying to catch a glimpse of what it was their mothers prayed against and longed for on Sundays.

"You used to run me."

"Yes."

"You used to tell me to go home."

"Yes."

"But I was home."

"I and I can never forgive meself for not recognising. Grief got in di way."

"Are you happy with all this? This must go against what you believe in, though we worship the same bible."

"Well, dere is religion and dere is culture, you understand? We honour we dead in order to realize life, dat is what me a try to show you. But, I and I don' like being roun di body; she no did deh. My queen gone. I and I is into life."

Pastor Collins stared into the lonely eyes of the old man. "Yes."

A hot tear rolled down his face, cooling as it reached his lips. The drums kept beating. They were getting louder now.

"Rarse!"

Mikey moved slowly. His age and religion made this difficult. But he was obligated, moved by his desire to do right. Pastor Collins brushed away the bush and leaves. He wanted nothing to get in the way of his vision of her.

Pastor Collins couldn't rock, couldn't sway or step to the drum. He stood motionless, held by the noise and prayer. He stared down at her. She seemed to be shrinking. He wondered if his passing would be this eventful. How come everyone still knew the songs? At first the townspeople watched, waited, hoped for the spectacle to provoke him, to draw out the hellfire God they lived with every Sunday. But he was still, recognising the cane church. He saw again the face of his supposed mother, as she had tried with everything she had to pull him back to her.

"Me tek you to protec you. What kind of life you tink you would be havin? Eee? Is where you tink you woulda be? Me will tell you, an heverybody here know it. You would be inna di groun. You hear me? Dead! You no know bout dem people. Please, lissen. It was di only way. I saw you laying dere and it was as if God tell me fi protect you. I had to get you weh from dem. You had to live, I had to save you."

He'd pulled her fingers from his shirt-front and walked away. She could have been right. Maybe he would have to be dead, but he would know who he was.

Mikey looked at him and saw a desperate boy who had waited his whole life to belong, and he felt scared that he couldn't do anything for him, anxious that he had too little time left. What if his heart gave out and he never got to know the boy? But then he would be with the only woman he ever truly loved. The thought wrapped him and his heart skipped beats.

"You don't know what it's like, lovin a woman and fearin her."

"That is all rubbish!"

"If it is, what we all doin here?"

"Did you look for me?"

"Well, no mus! Me look, me look, me look. I could not find you. She? She? She act like it was nuttin. Me? It brek me heart. Me tear di house apart, tear down me modder's house..."

"Your mother's?"

"Yes! She hated you modder. When you come along she hated you too. People tell me after she pass dat she go to the Lampis to help her – you understand?"

"That's..."

"Well, me no know how true it is, but she pass, alone and outta she mine when I was away. Praise the most high and mighty dat me wasn't there. Of dat, me is grateful."

Pastor Collins thought about his family, all of them. Not only did he suddenly have a father, but he also had, somewhere in him, the remnants of a desperate grandmother, desperate enough to try and magic him out of existence. He rubbed his hands together, trying to rub her out of himself.

"Dat is why me leave. I couldn't stand how Seduce could carry on and I could not."

"I remember my mother sent me to the mainland soon after you left. I didn't see you for years."

"Yes."

"Where were you?"

"Dis is what I'm comin to. I and I need to tell you sumtin."

Mikey stopped again and touched his arm. "Dere is some

tings a man mus only tell anodder man. Then and only then, may he get some peace."

Pastor Collins looked at the staff he had always seen Mikey with. His hand was like a part of the wood; they were the same smooth red-yellow brown.

"I and I kill a dead man once. When I and I first land on di Black Isle, di wind burn di hair inna me nose, so hot it was. I and I feel panic. Me fraid. As me an di other passengers walk off di ship, passengers from all over, dem black like me or brown, clear, but dem come from all ova, places me neva hear of. Dem hear about di fight an want to lend a hand. Dis was our time, mek me tell you, we was goin tek back what was ours.

"We walked, blinking – some of us been on dat ship fi weeks. I and I walk into town. Dat is what me say, *walk* into town. Back den, di Black man had to stoop, but when me reach di Black Isle, me jus tek me time an walk into town, head high. Nobody stop me, ask me what me doing dere, nuttin. Den when me get dere me realise why it so easy. Di town cover in bodies, black and white, together in death. Only two man me could see alive, at the other end of town, cloth over dem faces, moving through di dead. A cart, already high wid people, was being pulled along by a mean-looking donkey. Dese two men, wid no fear an no standards – dey pick watches, money, shoes – loaded di cart wid di bodies to be tek away an burn.

"I and I don't care bout the corpses. Hardly notice dem. I and I was still walking tall. You must know what dat means to a black man."

Pastor Collins did know and felt a sadness that placed him next to his father, watching the grave robbers, wondering at the future.

"Night was fallin, an den me realise dat nobody else was in di town. All me shipmate scatter, fearful of being out after nightfall an now dem safe indoors. I and I make myself mayor of death town. I went into bars and pour meself drinks. I went into shops dat back home I and I would have to wait until di white people finish first. Then me see him. A man so white it hard to believe dat him start life wid any colour at all. He was slumped over him counter, still protecting it, coins scatter all around him. I and I could not tell what had kill him till me turn him over and find di hole in him ches'. Flies rise up from di hole and di smell bring water to me eye. Me feel no pity. Jah know who dis man was, what him do, how many of us him kill or condemn, how many offspring he force into life. Is dead him dead. It was di first dead white man me ever see. Me bury a few, been paid a few shillings to carry dem coffin to dey final judgment, but dis was di first one me see. An me heart jus swell wid pride. Isn't dis why me come here, isn't dis why me lef Sed? Me start fi dash tings round di shop. Me no know why, me jus feel to stand up an dash tings. Don't even know what me dashing. Me just grab sumting an fling it. Den sumtin else. Me smash any glass or crockery dat leave. Me sweat wid joy. As me spin roun me see di ole farder, in one corner, crouch down, him hand trying to shield he head. Him look alive. When me see him me jump. When me gently push him, him fall, slump to di wall. Him face look old, but him eyes, wide wid shock, look young. Him look like he die of fright. Me heart feel for him. Had he died scared, fearin for his life and seeing di black man rise up? How did him feel? I and I drag him outside, an as me drag him down di steps one of him foot pull off. Di smell terrible. Me lay di grandfarder gentle on di ground. But me bury him, say a few words, and di hole me mek wid me hand, me fill up wid me hand."

Fear and dread hung around them. Pastor Collins thought about the dignity of a shallow grave.

"Me go back to di shop, fill me pockets wid whatever me could eat and was jus about to leave when me turn back. Me look round fi sumtin heavy, or sharp, except me couldn't find nuttin, so me pick up a piece of a plate or a tray, a long thin piece, and stab di white man. Just the once. No blood come forth, dat was long gone, spread like cold molasses over di floor. Me nuh know why I and I stab dis white man even though someone else tek him life. Dere me was, lookin pan him knowing dat he could never talk, he couldn't point me out to di police of dis place, could not hunt an run me down wid dog an horse, an have me swinging from a tree, or lash till di flesh fall away. No. So I and I kill a dead man an free meself."

Pastor Collins could feel himself sinking rapidly to the ground that just wouldn't come to meet him. He kept falling and falling.

"Seduce tink seh she is di law on death. True she see much of it. But me, me see death too. Not in her way but in mine. Standing over de white man body me catch sumtin in di corner of me eye, an when me look up it was a little mix-up girl, like Glory, she black but pale. She look dutty an fraid, her hair look solid on her head an her clothes tear up. She stare at me, den, looking down di street, she run. When me get to di doorway she long gone, but up di road me see why she run. Soldiers, a whole battalion, was marching towards me. Dem mostly white, a few blacks, talk into betraying demselves, at di front. When me see dem, dat hanging tree start fi beckon. When me look back into di shop, wid di dead white shopkeeper trying to preserve him money, dere was no way me could get out of it. Me run. Out di back of di shop, me run. Me tink me hear someone holla, but me wasn't goin to stop to fine out. Me run and keep on running till me legs buckle. When me stop it was coming to daybreak. When me look back me see smoke on di horizon."

Silence and sighs passed between them.

"Me tink bout you, Sed, me boat, Church, as me fine meself inna foreign landscape. I wanted to hear di rain, not see it. But me see it, like a stray cloud touchin di lan, and in between dere was di fire an smoke of a losin battle."

There was a strange awkward reality about it, as when land is reflected in water. As they walked and Pastor Collins listened, they caught up with the others. Mikey passed him back the pipe.

Collins looked again into the face lined with misery and joy and he wondered if he wanted more. The bush put him at ease. He was covered, protected from the sight of others. This place, which Hyacinth taught him to fear, had become a sanctuary. As they approached the fires that marked the circle containing Seduce and the drummers and as he saw the goat, nervous and knowing, being sprinkled with rum, he felt his soul soar up. Was this what it felt like to touch the hand of the creator? Could he be home?

The Cane Church

Loo

We watchin and waitin, til the waitin bore holes in we inside. We want dat she travel safe. We already mek dis journey, a long time ago, and never expec dat our flesh would live. We tired but we here, and we grateful. We feel di awe. Is when di laughter and drinkin ends dat the journey begin. We fi ever hopeful.

I and I wonder bout weself. When we eyes open we find life grow inside us. The honey left inside is turnin into true love, true life, beyond anyting dat any man can provide. But we mus not tink too much like dat or else we will turn into the other of us, who cannot look at man widout bile coming to our mouth. That's not for us. It waste our time.

Bless my bredder. Him more to me than he know, but him go always need protecting. His soul empty. Like a child, stranded on a rock where him trying to escape the tide, watchin the water rise to his fat likkle feet. Him go run? Him go swim? Lost boy, lost soul. We see in his eyes that him lookin for we. We go mek sure him find us.

"Loo?"

"Bredda."

"I… I don't know if I should be here, Loo… I…"

"Why?"

The drums nearly take his voice away. We see his ches' risin an fallin in time to them.

"Iyah, Iyah, Iyah!"

"Fire!"

"This is… I… feel sick."

"Here."

He drinks deep di wata and rum we give him.

"You know why you here, Son, you see dis before."

"How you know?"

"Be a witness, me bredda, we need you fi help sen her, she a part ah you too."

He get pull by a young girl, she drive him forward. He have him own journey to fine.

We have hips dat sway an long. We have eyes dat see an need. In a rush of fire, we know where we need to go. Come di cleansin fire. Our breaths combine. We eat di red earth.

"Sshh, sshh, listen, listen, listen to the land dat spawn us. We callin, we callin."

We in places dat fill us wid no joy. Why tings thus? Where is di joy? Di love an gravity dat should keep us weighted and tie to each other? Where are di people an family an di multiple of multiples dat should bind us? We nuh want be disappoint but still we are. We still like infant.

We in an out a here, dis pile a dirt we call home. Mus see weself as we is. Nanny was di only one dat saw us. Pain is a wondrous ting; it fill us with feelin and smells and sights and sounds. We own pain eat us like hungry fire. And nuttin matta, cept what we feelin. An life can go by. Love can go by. An still we pain is di only ting we can memba bout weself. But di pain of oddas? Di sound high an it echo long within us, even when we own pain long since gone. We memba Son pain, memba wiping away blood from him lip and giving him river water to wash all di pain away. He take di bowl a water, push me aside an go and wash behine di house. We don' have to look far. Di house know di secrets as much as we. One time, we found him tie to di mantrap outside di house. Him feet look burn an him eyes loss all dey humanness. Him look like animal. We was ever watchful, but could not find who hurtin we bredder. Then, one hot clear morning, Nanny say him mussa be send away an we know she protecting him and givin him life dat she feared would be wrench from him small body by we modder.

And see, how him respond to his callin. He's our witness and in his eyes all tings are seen and, maybe, maybe, dere comes healing afta dis.

Our fingers grow long an we clutch di bag wid di herbs in it. Sometimes, when we feel lost and alone, we wonder to take the herbs weself, but we know now dat we have a job to do.

…"Come, Nanny drink dis."

She eye flutter like small bird in a tree.

"What is it?"

"Tea."

"Bush tea?"

"Yes, Nanny"

We put di cup to she lip and pour a likkle in. Her eye on me and then she look out di window.

We gave her more and some fell down her chin. Di genkle breeze comin from di window stop.

"Galang." Afta a likkle while di fight fi breath seem to sekkle. Di struggle start to ebb. We rememba dis, for dis when di worl' slow dung, til it nearly stop, and deep in our souls an ache start.

"Tank you." She seh words me don't tink we ever hear she seh and then she close she eyes. When we check she gone, we run out di house, sleep in tree root and under di house bottom til we have to come back. Weselves are everliving and flow through each other. We knew dis was comin and yet now that it here, it feel strange. We feel… lost? Like a speech unspoken, or sumtin in the breeze, nuttin to latch onto, no one fi catch us but weself. And look dere! As we mout fulla dirt an everyting dat's in it, look! Dere! A shadow in di cane, jus as Nanny seh. Him move roun di edge, copyin birds inna di sky, roun an roun, til me cyant follow. It is nearly time. We shake we head. Is natral fi all tings to reach out, like a plant stretch toward di sun, but di stretchin has ourselves wear out. We thin with reachin, feel we bout to snap. But now, we have reach weself. Turned di stretchin in. Look at what is in us. See here, we have found sumting. Our body has a life in it, small an needful. She go mek di sky a different blue, di bird dem sing loud an strong. She in di smell ah tings. We know dat what we have is a gift for all dem dat know how fi use her. We know, widout di blink of an eye or a skippin of a heartbeat, dat she will bring us to our knees, tears will wet di ground for her, an we will willingly lose we life for the love of her. We know what moves us. It is love. She will be all of us.

On the way to the Cane church

Son

I have been to the cane church before. When Nanny went all those years ago I followed. It was a dark red night. The shadows formed no recognisable shapes and covered everything. Where are my shadows that attach me to this? I think Loo has them all.

Nanny took the long plait that for years had lived down her back and wound it round her head. It looked like a black and grey basket. On top of that she tied a piece of cloth, the brightest white I'd ever seen, tucking in any strays. She knew I was watching. Her movements were deliberate and slow so that I would remember them. She wrapped a green cloth around her waist, stepped out into the night and stood on the veranda, so I could keep up with her.

Long since, I could outrun her, could get up there before her, laugh in her face as she stumbled up the hill towards me. Even so, when the Lampis lift her out of the coffin, I half-expect her to beat them off, tell them bout dem backsides and climb out herself. But that life has gone. She looks so dead. When I was young, it seemed to me that she would never get old, frail, dependent, that she wouldn't, couldn't die. I'd heard the stories. Ours is a magical stock. I thought, as a child thinks, that she would always be here, a part of this place, a part of us.

For a moment, I didn't know where I was or why they were taking her up the hill. I was back on the veranda, watching Nanny as she breathed in the night air, breathed out unwanted memories. I don't know why I know that, but I do. She walked down the steps to the yard and stood motionless. I crept up behind her, thinking that the shadows would hide me. I hid by the chair reserved for guests to take the breeze on the side of the house where the hill falls slowly away towards the sea. She walked out, turned to the back of the yard and then started to climb. The hill seemed to help her up and try to stop me. It won't stop me now. Somebody's started a song. It sounds like a lament for home, but I have no home. I'm a stranger here.

Poking me, squeezing my arms, touching my head, twisting me, looking under my arms, sniffing at me, she'd catch Mama, in the middle of whatever she was doing, and say, "Dat bwoy, sen him away, he not lasting here." So, that was how I lived, under the threat of death without knowing what I had done or why I should die.

What is it about a woman that's born with the desire to kill man? What did we do so wrong?

I don't want to understand this ceremony. I don't want it to have anything to do with me, but… I feel the need to do something, be a part of it all.

When Nanny climbed the hill at the back of the house, she stopped at the clearing she called sacred. I watched from behind a tree. She sat down and I knew she was praying. It was where her Mama lay. So she said. And where she was conceived. She rocked gently and mumbled, then raised her voice to the sky. I got bored and thought about going home, but when I looked behind me, I didn't recognise anything and was afraid to walk all that way in the dark. When I looked at Nanny, I felt safe, though I didn't know where she was going or how the night would end. I was transfixed by the darkness and the light that shifted around her. Now, I am fascinated by the will of the Lampis, by the sudden knowledge that they are right or at least that they have the right.

They hold her delicately now, and carry her in a cloth of many greens. Sometimes, against the background of the hill, it looks as though she is floating and glimpses of her black body can be seen against the land and the hands that carry her. They follow the drummers and we follow them.

I was supposed to leave or die. That was my fate. Damned by the female belief in male stupidity. No one expected anything from me, except Loo, who loved me and cared for me more than Mama ever did or Nanny ever could. Even though she was younger than me, her spirit is older. She protected me from Nanny's disappointment and Mama's indifference. I don't think she knew what she was doing, she just did. She gave me her food, stubbornly stood in the way of blows and took some of them for me. It was a trial being brought up in a house of bitter women. Mama couldn't contain it within herself and when it burst out from her, it landed squarely on me. I was supposed to shrivel up. Instead, I took whatever was between my legs and ran to the mainland, to be lost in the sea of desperate black faces, the memory of home hanging over me.

Memories are merging. Back then Nanny rocked and rolled. She paused to let me see where she was heading and then strode forward. She walked in the night like a cat that could see in the dark. She walked and I followed. Every now and then she would stop, wait for me to catch up and then continue.

I felt for an instant that this was a moment awash with love and hope. I am not the man to see this and feel this easily. I am not that man. But that magical time, it was so believable. With the moon bright and high in the sky, it was believable that people were there who were not there, that trees moved, that more than we can see not only existed but moved our limbs and thoughts. I believed it all. Now, it feels stale and desperate.

There is nothing, was nothing, will always be nothing.

She kept walking. Soon my eyes grew used to the dark, the blackness that only lives in the countryside. There were lights up ahead, torches staked in the ground. The Lampis were there, all in white. I saw a young goat tied to a tree. Nanny stopped.

"We mus remember, for if our eyes forget, our souls will not." I knew she was talking to me, but we still played the game. I didn't try to work out what she meant. Even by then Loo and I made fun of her sayings. But now I know. I think I know. That night led me here. We remember everything, our bodies remember everything.

*

I look at the goat. It looks at me. The Lampis have started to dance and sing.

"We have hips dat sway an long. We have eyes dat see an

need. In a rush of fire, we know where we need to go. Come di cleansin fire. Our breaths combine."

Loo is sitting, mumbling and talking to whoever. She reaches out her hand and pulls at the dirt in front of her and she puts a handful in her mouth. All the time talking.

"Sshh, sshh, listen, listen, listen to the land that spawn us. We callin, we callin."

She sways. Her lives within her have already lived this. Mikey has found an old leg and joined in. The Lampis jump and dance and turn their bodies into trees and rivers and mountains. They become the bush, as if it had always been so.

The birds have stopped singing and it was only then that I notice that they have been singing at all, into the darkness, loud and sure.

"Come the coming."

"In all the ways."

"Know the knowing."

"In all the ways."

The song gathers up the lost souls and holds them close to the beating heart of the world.

We reach the cane church, a large, perfect circle cleared in the cane. Leaves low and dry. We walk like ants in a forest of everything that was bigger than us. The cane is tall and unbending. We keep walking, as I did as a child, still following my grandmother. Black birds swoop above our heads. I stop. A shiver runs through me. I can't help but think how many of us have died here. The air is thick, warm and soupy. I sweat cold water, which makes me shiver more. Some townspeople can go no further and have turned back. Some just stand still, blocked by fear or memories that their bodies still cling to. They can't let themselves be engulfed again.

The drummers make a tight circle around Seduce's body, they face each other and start her journey. They sway, shuffle along, not breaking the circle and shout prayers and compliments to the spirits.

I feel excluded, but unable to be anywhere else. This is for women, not men, and although all the drummers are men, I get the feeling that they are all in her service. Maybe more of her discarded children, sons of men she knew. I look at the reddish soil as it covers my shoes. Loo moves from foot to foot like a giant white turtle. Her eyes glisten, the curve of her neck draws the moonlight away from the shadows. I have to keep quiet, my voice would not be heard here. Mikey sits on the ground, with help from people he is starting not to recognise.

"Rest, rest, quiet yourself. We feel you and hear you and are you. Come, tek she weh."

My uncle hovers near him. Also looking like an alien in his own land.

Seduce rocked with the rest of the Lampis and her spirit thought that knowledge was a terrible thing, dat people who know too much, loose dem reason. She look up and thought she felt a mountain in the distance.

I was scared of the Lampis back then. They seemed such huge women that they blotted out everything behind them. I sat in the bush and watched them, listened to Nanny singing to herself. She had a bottle; even from where I was I could smell the rum. Rum lives in our souls. We were stolen for it, died for it, and how many of us drink our flesh and bone to abandon now! The Lampis knew. The Lampis drank deeply, and so did Nanny, then they each in turn spat out: East, West, South, North. A little rum caught me in the shadows and I felt its sting on my face. They shouted the names of people I didn't know, lost babies, men, daughters, lovers. They danced. Nanny put a glass of rum on her head and bowed to everyone who was there. I thought, but wasn't sure, that she had bowed to me. Then she spun and spun, not spilling a drop, her skirts rising up showing her dark legs quivering against the white material. When she finished, she spat on the goat. It was agitated, tried to free itself from the rope. Then Nanny stood over it. The drums and the bleating of the goat got louder. Some Lampis fell to the floor, screaming, writhing as if tortured by unseen devils. They hit themselves, scratched at themselves. Then Nanny picked up her machete and straddled the goat and cut its throat. It didn't die straight away, but stood crying. The blood was collected by the

Lampis and distributed for them to drink. I had seen dead animals before, had tortured and killed many frogs and birds in childish games. It was the noise that held my terror. The noise of the goat as it was untethered and let loose to walk and bleed where it might and cry aimlessly into the night. It looked in my direction. The Lampis cried too.

"Boy!"

I didn't hear her come up behind me and stand over me. I felt the shirt around my neck being yanked up. I thought it was a duppy had hold of me and started to scream, flashed my arms about. It was Nanny. She boxed me swiftly.

"Get out of here. This is no place for you."

Her breath was hot with rum and goat's blood. I didn't recognise her eyes. I tried to run, my legs kicked and sprang from my body, but she held me.

"Shall we cut you t'roat next?"

Pee came down my leg. Finally she let go and I ran as fast as I could, branches grasping at my clothes and face. A sense of shame pinched my eyes. The laughter of the Lampis chased me and I knew that she had let me follow her only so she could catch me. All women were traitors and I cursed them as I ran, wishing that I could run across the water.

I found a small clearing, smaller than this one and sat down amongst its roots, as big as the trees they grounded. My breath burned as it poured out of me. I put my head on my knees and cried. Long sobs that joined the other night noises. When I'd stopped and could see, there was a calabash of water near my feet. I drank and then stumbled home.

I see Loo stand and hold up the small bag that has been resting on her hip. The drummers and dancers stop suddenly, watching Loo, and then continue to move again. Every movement seems to start from the centre of the body and move up and out. I remember this from before.

"Come, tek you place. Dere is room for everyone. Come!"

The Lampis pull people from where they stand, swaying and encouraging. I feel a burning in my pocket. The white hankerchief. I take it out and bend over her and tie it around her head. A circle of moving prayer starts, little puffs of red smoke gathering at our feet. A wind comes from the sea and moves the cane around us. I look at Nanny, small and black in her shroud of green and wish that she wasn't there any more. That she is wherever she wants to be.

The drums take my legs and shift them along. I'm in the circle, next to my sister. The red of the sky and earth goes and all that is left is green. I can hear the noise of joy and sadness, peace and praise. We have all forgotten that if we are caught it could be a prison sentence. Loo dances next to me, her eyes closed, yet I know she can see me. Around we go. I find myself again and again at the same spot, staring into Nanny's body. I find a chicken in my hands. I hold it flapping above my head. Everyone stops and looks at me. Then we start again. This time the drummers get quicker. Sweat runs down my back. I don't know when the head comes off in my hands but a great cry goes up, and I'd looked for that sound coming. Blood pours into the calabash Loo is holding. She blesses it, takes it to the Lampis. They sing, old voices, old hands, holding onto our present.

Another body is next to me and I hold onto it. Feel the curve of a spine, the pushing of hips and I hold onto it. Her arms circle me, a woman whose face I don't know and I hold on. It feels good. And when I feel I might fall, the woman takes off a scarf from her waist and puts it around me. Sweat falls in my eyes. She leads me around the body of Nanny until I can't go on.

A great blaze comes up from her and surrounds us. The fire is cold, even and short lived. Some people scream.

"Quiet youself. Come di cleansin fire."

The Lampis control them and when they realise they are not burning, they sing. I close my eyes. I do not want to see.

"Let it go, Son." Loo is behind me, her hand on my shoulder, helpin me move. She hands me the calabash, and salt and rum fill my mouth.

The air bends and trees move, a branch touches my shoulder. Old eyes reflect mine. It can only be him. Coming to help me.

The grip gets tighter, I'm still moving, the cane holds me and is gone.

The sun is black and the heat is black with the look of oil. It opens pores to let the light in and the dark out, to see yuhself and you kin. Heat, dark heat, hot, cold, hot, hot, burning, not burning, opens my eyes. I can't... stuck, like hands across my face... Going to be sick, sick... bread in my throat won't come, will come... fish and bread make hot soup in my throat. Blood is pullin me, dancing in me. Am I dying? Dead? Will I ever be able to open my eyes? What will I see? Sick, guts hurting, my thing is alive, not for touching, touch it, touch me, reach there and touch, touch, cool wind from sea, stroking cold flames in front of me, sick, purple, open, we, open, we see, open, we see, we see di ships, fingers, death and water, ropes tight round we necks, metal biting we flesh, blood in we eyes, we see, we see weselves.

More wind this time from the mountains and as we open our eyes a great black bird flies from the fire and Nanny is gone.

Seduce

See me yah, toh, toh, toh. Tek some duppy spit inna you food. Me hope it choke you. No, wait. Me nuh want none ah you near me, you hear me? None ah you. Me nuh want none ah you any place me deh. Me nuh want yuh fi see me, yuh hear? Me can see you, to backside, me can see all a you, you dutty nasty low dung neagah. Yes, me seh neagah yes, for dat is what you is, don't it, don't it? A neagah people like all a we, but yuh nuh know dat, yuh nuh see what you a do, yuh nuh see is who grave you a step pan, a no me, a you mumma an poppa, a no me. Yuh all here fi send me to hell. Curse you, curse you! You here fi check me dead an kick-up you foot pan me grave – a no me; or wash you mout pan me business – a no me; you hear what me seh – a no me. Yuh come fi look inna me dead face and watch di flesh harden. Yuh like di worms dem, already a lick dem lips, starin at me ches' fi see if life still a fight in deh. Yuh come fi look roun me house, pass you nasty puss eyes over me tings, to mumble in sof tones, but really you have a heart fill wid joy an celebration, yuh hear what me seh. Yuh come to watch who talking to who, who secretly smilin at who, to arrange to meet up later an follow di direction di man trap pointin, up di way deh. Yuh make up noise inna me name, to see who is wearing who, which one a dem a grieve and which one a rejoice. A no me, you hear, a no me, a you mama an poopa. Is me you come lookin fah, is me, an to backside you fine me, like dat smell under you armpit, you fine me like a tic under you skin, buryin in the hole of you eyelash, under you nails, like di dirt a someone else, deep, dark deep inna you ears, inna you cratches. Dat's me. I am di spring dat flow troo all a you, I am di well dat has collected all a you, I am the tree on the ridge dat fight wid di night sky fi de moon.

I am di leaves an branches, plant in di red soil, wash up on yuh shores. I am whispering troo yuh press hair. I catch yuh renk stinkin breath inna me han. I trowing it all back to you. Come den, mek me tek you where you a go, mek me show you what you need to know, right inna me cratches, watch me shit out you guilt an collec you misery. Come forward, all dose dat can feel me, all dose dat can hear me, all dose dat want to touch me, see me yah, see me yah. Come den, beg yuh come.

Souls

The day opens her legs to let the night in. It moves from a dark lilac to bottomless purple. Waiting for a moment to adjust your eyes, against your skin is a smooth coolness. By the light of the moon, in the distance you can make out a large structure that almost blots out the horizon. You can't tell if it's a building or something more natural, a shadow, a greater darkness just recognisable against the blackness. Clinging to the edges you can see movement.

The souls sail around, chit-chatting and remembering nothing. Souls are like that. Visiting so many places, so many people they very soon forget where they have just been. They only know where they are going; when they are there they are already starting to forget. They wheeled overhead and cried loud into the dark, feathers reflecting moonlight, sharp eyes watchful. They bustle and nudge each other, some getting angry about the lack of space. A few circle ahead, waiting for one to go back. Sometimes they nip and scratch. They know they are only there for a short time, so they want to make the most of it. Some are bigger than others, some are quiet but most are loud and for those that can hear, the squawking can be heard for miles. Their long claws grip tightly to the perches and the small eyes look as if they are trying to remember. A gap on the branch becomes free and suddenly several souls race for it. A fight breaks out, as often happens at these times.

They wait. They never know when it's about to happen, just a strong tugging that takes them back, through the light and the dark and the cold and the heat and finally again the cold. Like mothers they forget the pain. A small one manages to beat some others off the perch. This one has been wanting the pull back. Wants to go. Looking, waiting, watching. Others are squawking, loudly.

She pays them no mind, she has squawks of her own she's not ready to let go of. Sounds and trills that belong to her. She is tired but ready to get back.

She has flown many miles and her wings ache. She stretches them as far as they can go, shoving other souls out of the way and making them screech with annoyance. She wears the scars of many fights. They have seen her before and she has seen them. There are no strangers. She looks forward to a short rest and wants no wings, no claws, no beaks in her face. As she folds herself into herself and tries to shut out the noise, she shuts her eyes and thinks of her old time and sighs at the thought of her new time. She hears the old souls fighting with the new. The scratching, the pecking, the belching and the farting. She nibbles at her shoulder. She did not want time to let her rest. She was waiting for the pulling, the sweet release of life again. There is no room, there is never any room. Then the restlessness takes over, which is when more fighting starts. Her eyes finally shut. Her time has gone and will come again. She has no choice but to sit and sleep, occasionally pushing and pecking the others out of the way. And wait.

ABOUT THE AUTHOR

Desiree Reynolds was brought up in Clapham, London to Jamaican parents. She told her Mum, at about eight years old, that she was going to write a book and has been writing ever since. The early works continue to be hidden in a drawer. She started her writing career as a freelance journalist for the *Jamaica Gleaner* and the *Village Voice*. She left school as quickly as she could and went to South Thames and Westminster College. Having completed two degrees, she has been a shop assistant, youth worker and an editor. She has gone on to write film scripts, poetry and short stories. She continues to work as a journalist, writing book and film reviews. She is a broadcaster, creative writing workshop facilitator, DJ and mentor. She has had several short stories published in various publications. Desiree is inspired by internal landscapes and collective memory. *Seduce* is her first novel. She is currently working on a collection of short stories, based on growing up in South London and a novel about the collapse of the plantation system in the Caribbean.

Find her online at http://desireereynolds.co.uk/

ALSO FROM PEEPAL TREE

Curdella Forbes
Ghosts
ISBN: 9781845232009; pp. 182; pub. 2012; Price: £8.99

The circumstances of their brother's violent death inflicts such a wound on his family that its four oldest sisters feel compelled to come together to write, tell or imagine what led up to it, to unravel conflicting versions for the benefit of the younger generation of the huge Pointy-Morris clan.

From the richly distinctive voices of the writer Micheline (Mitch), who could never tell a straight truth, the self-contained and sceptical Beatrice (B), the visionary and prophetic Evangeline (Vangie), and the severely practical Cynthia (Peaches), the novel builds a haunting sequence of narratives around the obsessive love of their brother, Pete, for his dazzling cousin, Tramadol, and its tragic aftermath.

Set on the Caribbean island of Jacaranda at different points in a disturbing future, *Ghosts* weaves a counterpoint between the family wound and a world caught between amazing technological progress and the wounds global warming inflicts on an agitated planet.

In a lyrical flow between English and Jamaican Creole, *Ghosts* catches the ear and gently invades the heart. Love enriches and heals, but its thwarting is revealed as the most painful of emotions. Yet if deep sadness is at the core of the novel, there are also moments of exuberant humour.